The power of memory...

"Do you remember that time I tried to jump off the roof of the toolshed?"

"You were such a picture. Sometimes I can still see you poised on top of that roof, with no doubt in the world that you could fly."

"Is that why," Jo Ella asked softly, "you always call me your little bird?"

"No," Cam answered slowly. "That's from something I read somewhere... about not being able to say a bird belongs to you until you let it go and it flies back to you of its own free will." Then he smiled at her and shrugged a little. "Silly, I guess."

Jo Ella met Cam's gaze, a strange and wonderful contentment stealing through her. She lifted her hand and lightly touched the small scar, just above his temple, where the falling branch had struck him so many years ago. She whispered, "No. Not silly at all."

Books by Rebecca Flanders

HARLEQUIN AMERICAN ROMANCE

6—A MATTER OF TRUST
24—BEST OF FRIENDS
41—SUDDENLY LOVE
51—GILDED HEART
58—SECOND SIGHT
66—DESERT FIRE
74—THE THIRD TIME
83—DAYDREAMS
100—OPEN HANDS
105—RAINBOWS AND UNICORNS

HARLEQUIN INTRIGUE

1—THE KEY
8—SILVER THREADS
13—EASY ACCESS

HARLEQUIN PRESENTS

632—MORNING SONG
666—FALKONE'S PROMISE

HARLEQUIN ROMANCE

2623—A MODERN GIRL

Open Hands

REBECCA FLANDERS

Harlequin Books

TORONTO • NEW YORK • LONDON
AMSTERDAM • PARIS • SYDNEY • HAMBURG
STOCKHOLM • ATHENS • TOKYO • MILAN

ABOUT THE AUTHOR

Rebecca Flanders is a native of Georgia who pursues her writing career with great enthusiasm. She has been the author of several American Romances, and each successive one shows more of her diverse writing ability. In what little spare time Rebecca has, she enjoys oil painting and both listening to and writing music.

Published April 1985

First printing February 1985
Second printing July 1985

ISBN 0-373-16100-X

Printed In Canada

Chapter One

Slowly, one by one, Jo Ella Cable uncurled the fingers that had formed into unconscious fists. The tension that had tied her entire body into one giant knot was so static she was certain the woman across the desk must feel it. Jo Ella did not want to give her prospective employer the satisfaction of knowing how anxious she was; she could not afford to give the other woman the upper hand. She tried to relax her face muscles into nonchalance and tried not to hope for much. She tried not to think how many interviews she had been on in the past three weeks, and most of all she tried not to anticipate the answer she knew was coming.

Mrs. Wesley was not much older than Jo Ella; she had seemed kind and sympathetic throughout the interview. Yesterday she had given Jo Ella the full-scale tour of the hospital and had even bought her lunch; when she had asked Jo Ella to come back today for a final decision, Jo Ella knew she had a chance. Not once had Jo Ella's past been mentioned. And that was what worried her.

Jo Ella tried to think positively. The hospital was

short on nurses—what hospital in the country wasn't?—and it would be hard to turn down an R.N. with Jo Ella's qualifications. She was administrative material; she only had two credits to go on her M.A. degree. She was qualified in many specialities, and her experience was vast. She was single, with no prospects, which meant she had no personal life to interfere with on-call duty. And she was also desperate, which was perhaps Jo Ella's biggest asset of all. There was a chance.

Then Mrs. Wesley looked up with a smile and Jo Ella knew there was no chance. She was already reaching for her purse as the woman spoke. "I'm going to be frank with you, Jo Ella," she said kindly. How many times had Jo Ella heard those words in the past three weeks? She knew what they presaged. "Your qualifications are excellent, and if it were up to me I'd hire you in a minute. We'd be lucky to have you, but—"

"It was a board decision," Jo Ella finished for her. The smile she had meant to be sarcastic was merely weak. "Well, thank you for your time, Mrs. Wesley."

The woman looked, for a moment, truly sorry. She was in an odd position. They were sisters under the skin, and a part of her understood and sympathized with Jo Ella's position. "There, but for the grace of God, go I" was in her expression. But another part, perhaps the stronger part, tried very hard not to look at Jo Ella, and the scandal that surrounded her, with loathing and fear. It was as though Jo Ella Cable in and of herself had tainted the entire sacred institution of nursing, or as though the professional leprosy she had might be contagious. Perhaps Mrs. Wesley did, indeed, sense what a fine line divided her position from Jo Ella's and did not want to think about how easily she herself might slide over that line.

"Jo Ella," she said gently, "before you go, do you mind if I ask you a question?"

Jo Ella looked at her, not rising.

Mrs. Wesley said quietly, almost reluctantly, "Have you considered... perhaps your days of usefulness as an R.N. are over? You're not too old to make a career change. There are other medically related fields that don't require patient contact. Have you thought about going into another line of work?"

Jo Ella's smile was a little bitter. "Another line of work," as though she were a telephone operator or a seamstress at a garment factory or a door-to-door salesperson—all of which occupations were beginning to sound more and more inviting.

They never asked whether or not Jo Ella was guilty. She wondered what she would tell them if they did.

Jo Ella hooked the strap of her purse over her shoulder and stood up, her smile making a surface effort to thank the woman for what could very well have been genuine concern. And she said, "Now may I ask you a question?" She paused at Mrs. Wesley's inquiring lift of the eyebrow. "Would you really have hired me," Jo Ella asked softly, "if it had been up to you?"

She did not wait for an answer. She didn't have to. The answer was mingled with shame and guilt in the other woman's eyes.

The glare of the sun jolted Jo Ella's eyes and every stone step jarred her spine as she made her way out to the hospital parking lot. The nurses who came up the steps in groups of two and three, talking and laughing among themselves, represented a secret society to which Jo Ella had once belonged but did no longer. The entire hospital atmosphere seemed alien and antagonistic toward her. It felt good to take a breath of clean, warm air and rid herself of the cloying sense of defeat that had permeated the little office in which she had sat for the past forty-five minutes. It felt good to be out under the Texas sky and away from the enclosure of four walls. She could make herself believe for one moment that the world was full of possibilities and she was free to pick and choose among them, that nothing could be as dire as it seemed right now.

But that was a fleeting comfort. Right now things seemed about as dire as they were ever going to get.

The car had absorbed and retained the warmth of the sunshine through its rolled-up windows, and a blast of heat hit Jo Ella as she opened the door. She left the door open as she started the engine, letting it idle until the air conditioner began spewing forth a faint stream of cooler air. Then she closed the door and slammed the car into gear, and made her way none too carefully out of the parking lot.

Jo Ella had to think about what Mrs. Wesley had said, and she tried not to let it make her angry. Why was she killing herself over this thing? Couldn't she take a hint? She would never work in nursing again, no matter what the courts said, no matter what the licensing board said...and why was she letting it matter so much? Why fight it?

The woman was right. Jo Ella was twenty-seven years old, young by most standards. She could use the administrative and clerical skills she had acquired through nursing as a basis for a new career, and the possibilities were almost endless. Of course, it wasn't exactly the best of times to be on the job market, but Jo Ella was a fighter; she could make it.

And that was precisely what made her so angry. She was a fighter, and she did not like to lose.

Mentally, Jo Ella counted the bills left in her wallet. It was not an encouraging picture. Did she dare try to stay here a few more days and arrange some more interviews? Her common sense challenged her, what was the point? But another, more forceful part of Jo Ella did not see how she could face going back home in defeat. And for a moment she was tempted just to keep on driving, past the motel, past the Dallas city limits, just to keep going east until her money ran out. What she would do then she had no idea. But at least, for a while, she would be doing something. She would be moving.

But she didn't. She turned her dusty Honda into the motel parking lot and switched off the ignition. Then she just sat there for a moment, with the sun beating down on the roof and rapidly eating up the cool air, and she felt the weight of failure bow her shoulders and spread its poisonous tendrils slowly toward the center of her soul.

The irony of the entire situation struck her. She had fought, all right, and won the biggest battle of her life. She had survived eight months of nearly going mad with worry, waiting for the trial. She had faced the hostility of friends and neighbors and the humiliation of losing her job. She had watched her co-workers desert her when she needed them most. She had lived with nightmares and terror and the burden she had placed upon her family. She had survived the awful publicity during the two weeks of the trial, and her heart had almost broken when it got to the point that her mother was ashamed to walk the streets of the town in which she had lived all her life. And then . . . she had won. She had been acquitted. The courts said she was innocent, the state of Texas returned her license to practice nursing. But what had she won? A lifetime of stigma and a career that would never recover from the blow public opinion had dealt it. When the trial was over, Jo Ella had thought she had put the worst behind her. Now she had to admit it was only beginning.

With a grim set to her lips, Jo Ella squared her shoulders and got out of the car. She did not know what she was going to do, but she wasn't giving up yet. She couldn't afford to.

The telephone was ringing when she unlocked the door to the air-conditioned motel room. She hesitated a long time before answering, her spirits falling, if possible, even further. No one knew how to reach her except her mother, and Jo Ella didn't think she could face the sound of her mother's cheerful voice . . . not today, not now.

Stabbed with sudden guilt, Jo Ella berated herself for a coward and went over to the phone.

"Hello, little bird," a pleasant masculine voice drawled into her ear. "When did you fly in?"

Jo Ella sank to the bed, a sensation like sun-kissed honey flowing through her limbs and oozing into the darkened corners of her mind. It was as though some god had smiled on her, sending her exactly what she needed at precisely the moment she needed it most. "Cam," she said softly, and it was only an echo of the syllable that seemed to have taken up the beat of her pulse, pushing life-giving hope and memories of joy through her veins. *Cam*.

She felt her lips curving into a smile that was as open and unaffected as the light in a child's eyes on Christmas morning, and she spoke more clearly into the receiver. "How did you know where to find me?"

"Elementary, my dear girl. Your mother called my mother, who promptly called me—the old jungle grapevine. I won't mention how hurt I am that you've been here two days and haven't once thought about calling me, but I will mention that my mother's heart is broken. She's been sobbing into her lasagna all day, and if you expect to get out of this town alive, you'd better agree to have dinner with her tonight."

Jo Ella laughed. "Soggy lasagna?"

"Getting soggier by the minute. I won't tell you what happened to the fatted calf she killed yesterday when she heard you were in town. We'll be having sandwiches out of that sucker for the next month."

Jo Ella choked on laughter that started to make her side ache. "Don't do this to me, Cam," she warned.

There was a silence, and now his voice was serious. "Why didn't you call, Joey?"

Jo Ella took a long breath and released it very slowly through her teeth, the laughter dying in her throat. Why hadn't she called? What could it have cost her to pick up the phone and dial the number of an old friend, or even his mother—the only people she knew in town?

"Complicated question, Cam," she said quietly.

"Care to tell me about it over dinner?"

She hesitated. "Did your mother really make lasagna?"

"I don't know—I can call and find out. Or would you rather be alone?"

She thought about Cam; his long brown hands, his warm hazel eyes, the quirky smile and the way he had of laughing deep in his throat. She said softly, "Yeah. Tonight I'd rather be alone."

"Okay. How's the food at the motel restaurant?"

"Canned, frozen and overcooked."

"Sounds great. I'll meet you there in half an hour."

Jo Ella smiled. "Right. See you then."

Cameron Scott was the only person in the world to whom Jo Ella did not have to explain what she meant when she said "alone."

Chapter Two

Cameron had always thought Jo Ella Cable was the gutsiest woman he had ever known. And probably, though his experience was by no means limited, the most fascinating.

When she was three and he was six, he had caught her perched upon the back of the meanest bull in the pasture, shouting "Giddap," and tugging at its horns as though it were no more than the friendly old St. Bernard that used to take the kids on rides around the front yard. How she had gotten up there no one to this day knew; how she had survived the experience was generally accredited to the intervention of a host of guardian angels. The youngest of seven, with four brothers and two sisters, Jo Ella had learned at an early age to fight for survival, but it was more than that—not only had she held her own in a crowded family, she had soon begun to outshine them.

No challenge was ever too great, no dare unmet—and Jo Ella's brothers, along with Cameron and his brother, provided plenty of them. She was the first one to climb the creaking apple tree to the very top. She was the only one ever to spend the night alone in what was locally rumored to be a haunted house. She emerged the next morning sleepy and covered with cobwebs, but otherwise totally unaffected. She rode her skateboard for two miles down the center lane of the highway. Sometimes Cameron shuddered when he thought of those days.

When she was eight and he was eleven, her favorite game had been diving from the barn loft into the fragrant piles of soft hay below. Though Cameron never demurred in the other games, that was one thing he had never been able to make himself do. It looked so high up there, the chances of missing the haystack or bouncing off and cracking his skull against the hard wooden floor enormous, and he just could not picture himself walking up to the edge of the platform and stepping off into thin air. But he watched Jo Ella, day after day, with a sort of hypnotic fascination. Often his heart was in his throat, often he wanted to call out to her at the last minute and stop her—after all, he was three years older and should have known better—but he never did. Just as Cameron had never learned to like hunting, he felt that restraining Jo Ella would be like cutting down a wild thing in the prime of its life.

Sometimes he could still see her, poised at the edge of the loft, sunshine streaming through the window and catching particles of dust in the air, bits of straw caught in her braids and blending with the colour of her hair, cheeks flushed with the heat of a summer day. He could hear the indolent humming of a bee and taste the fragrance of barnyard hay, and he could see himself standing below her, so small against the vastness of sky and roof that framed her. He could see the intensity of concentration on her face and the arch of her body as she pushed off, and she seemed to be poised there, in his memory, between earth and sky, a creature of the air with her braids streaming behind her and her arms flung out to touch the wind. He supposed that was when he first began to love her.

The two families had grown up together on neighboring spreads that were too small to be called ranches, too unproductive to be considered working farms. One by one Jo Ella's siblings went off to college or the military or to marriage, but things were never dull around the Cable household until Jo Ella herself moved away. Cameron's brother, Burt, was drafted and returned home with a pilot's license; Cameron joined the Coast Guard and saw much more of the world than he had expected to in four years. The two families wandered in and out of each other's lives; meeting at weddings and graduations and births, occasionally at Christmas and, sadly, at the funerals of both their fathers.

Jo Ella's mother had taken a little house in town, close to the residence of one of her daughters.

Burt and Cameron had opened a helicopter charter service in Dallas and moved their mother to a house in the Colony two years later. And Jo Ella was making a fair start on her goal of living in every major city in the world. No one ever knew at any given moment precisely where she was—except Cameron. They kept in touch. They floated in and out of each other's lives like two bits of chaff carried on crisscrossing wind currents; they touched and separated and never knew when or where they would meet again...just knowing they would.

That was why it disturbed Cameron that Jo Ella had not contacted him throughout this whole mess. He had had to learn of her troubles through his mother, who had persistently pried the story out of Jo Ella's mother some months after the event. Cameron had written Jo Ella a letter offering a shoulder to lean on and an ear to listen, but she hadn't answered it, so he did not follow up with a telephone call. He knew that there were times when the only thing Jo Ella asked from anyone was space, and he knew this was one of those times. He only wished she could have allowed him to help.

Cameron arrived at the motel restaurant early—he had not told Jo Ella that he was only ten minutes away when he called. If she had not answered her phone, he would have gone directly to her door; if she had not answered her door, he would have waited until she did. It was early for dinner, and Cameron sat at a window table in the nearly empty restaurant, watching people come and go until he saw the one face he had been waiting for.

The flax-colored braids had darkened and been shorn to a casual cap of fluffy light brown, a fly-away, little-care hairstyle that was trimmed neatly around the ears, winged to a point just above her collar in back, and full and bouncy on top. The dark-brown eyes were still the same, as were the china-doll nose she had always hated and the full curving lips that could create the most delightful dimple when she smiled or the most formidable pout when she was displeased. Her petite figure was the same—though perhaps a little lighter than Cameron remembered it—and so was her assertive, almost militant stride. Cameron had always said she had the funniest walk he had ever seen—shoulders back, chin out, short legs eating up ground like a tank on a seek-and-destroy mission, a way of walking totally at odds with her dainty, feminine build. She walked as though she saw herself six inches taller and thirty pounds heavier and could at any moment be expected to leap over tall buildings in a single bound.

She smiled and waved as she spotted him through the window, but no dimple appeared this time. Her face looked thinner, Cameron noticed upon closer inspection, and he did not like those hollow, mauve circles under her eyes. That this had been rough on her went without saying, and he was glad she had come to Dallas when she did.

Jo Ella slipped into the chair opposite him and felt the slow warmth of familiarity and relief steal over her with his smile. She would not have believed how good it could be simply to see the face of a friend. Lazy hazel eyes that welcomed her, a lean brown face that held no accusation or suspicion, strong shoulders that could carry the weight of the world if asked and never once complain. Cam. Dear Cam.

"Hiya, friend," she said softly, and he winked at her.

"Long time no see," he replied. "You look like hell."

"Makes sense," she agreed negligently, running her fingers through her tousled hair as she settled back. "Since that's where I've been for the past few months."

"It's a rough old world, isn't it?" he offered gently, and she simply nodded. The understanding that passed from one pair of eyes to the other needed no further words.

"So." Cam leaned back and stretched his long denim-clad legs beneath the table. The tip of his boot brushed Jo Ella's ankle, and she tucked her feet beneath the rung of her chair. She was used to making room for Cam. "Any luck with the job hunting?"

Jo Ella made a wry face. "What do you think?"

He looked at her thoughtfully for a moment. "I think," he decided, "we eat first and talk later. I didn't have any lunch."

Jo Ella shot him a grateful look and felt the last of the day's tension slide from her. Cam would know that the last thing she felt like talking about right now was her problems. They would have to be talked about, it was true, but she could handle it better with a buffer between the awful day and a verbal review of it. Right now what she wanted to do was forget it all for a while, and that was why Cam was here.

"How's your mom?" she asked as Cameron procured menus.

"Feisty as ever." He glanced over the menu. "Looks like we would have done better to have stayed at home and had TV dinners."

"Don't be so picky. It's nutritious. How about Burt and Mary, and the kids?"

"Fat and sassy. At least Mary and the kids are. She's pregnant again, you know."

"No, I didn't." Jo Ella looked up, flowing easily into hometown gossip about normal people and their normal lives, escaping for a much-needed rest into someone else's world.

They talked about Cam's family and Cam's business and Cam's life, they ate tasteless roast beef and wilted salad, and Jo Ella let the events of the past year drift away from her and be cleansed in the stream of familiarity and comfort. The sun was setting over Cam's shoulder, and the reddish light cast capricious shadows over his face, playing in his hair with little sparks and flames and glints of gold. Cam was a large man, but Jo Ella rarely remembered him as anything other than a boy. The surprise of seeing him affected her as it always did, even though he had been a grown man for ten years now. And that, of course, was it. For a while, until the newness wore off, Jo Ella would have to get used to seeing him as a man again.

He was very good-looking. His size alone attracted a fair share of female attention, but he was fortunate enough to have the grace of bearing and the facial features to go along with it, so that one was not disappointed on second glance. His shoulders were broad and straight and looked good encased in the faded denim work jacket he wore tonight. His arm muscles were not overdeveloped, but kept in shape nicely by the normal manual labor he did. That was important, because, had he been vain, a man with Cam's natural endowments could easily have gone overboard in developing his physique.

Cam had the strongest neck Jo Ella had ever seen. It was broad and columnar, and when viewed by itself it almost seemed to dwarf the rest of him, but of course his body was in perfect proportion, a natural link between the definitive shape of a masculine face and the breadth of a well-built torso. The sight of his bared throat, the heavy dip of his collarbone, the slight motion of his Adam's apple in low conversation, always tantalized Jo Ella with the desire to put her hands around his neck, just to see if her linked fingers could circle its circumference. Of course she never did. Not any more.

Despite his size and his unmistakable masculinity, there was nothing intimidating about Cam. It wasn't that he was unaware of the appeal he held for the opposite sex—he knew exactly what his charms were and he knew how to use them when it suited him—it was simply that, most of the time, he didn't care. He did not ooze sex appeal. He was not a master of smoldering glances or provocative stances. He was just a regular guy. And there was something about his face—a softness there that belied its strong shape, a gentleness about the mouth and an intelligence and perception in the eyes that suggested a poet more than a cowboy. He was an easy person to talk to.

Gradually Jo Ella became aware that Cameron was no longer talking but simply looking at her in the same quiet, assessive way in which she had been looking at him, and she suddenly wondered what he was remembering. Her own memories began to wander down forbidden trails and she wondered if, perchance, he was having the same thoughts... but the speculation threatened to make her blush, and she forcefully dismissed it.

The gentle smile in his eyes revealed nothing more than the concern of one friend for another. "So, my little bird," he said softly, "you've landed yourself in a real mess this time. What are you going to do?"

Jo Ella sighed, shaking her head slightly. It was not so much the meal as Cameron's simple presence that had fortified her, and she felt she could face a few realities now. "I don't know, Cam," she admitted. "I don't even know why I thought I could just pick up my life and go on after the trial. I guess thinking that I could, though, was the only thing that got me through it."

Cam looked at her thoughtfully. "Okay," he said. "Let's get down to some cold, hard facts. You got a rough break. It could have been any nurse in the hospital who was with Bobby Williams the night he died, but it just happened to be you. You did the best you could and it wasn't good enough, and you got yourself tangled up in some messy legalities. And even though you proved your innocence to the satisfaction of the courts, hospitals can't take a chance on involving themselves in any kind of scandal. So how broken up are you going to be if you can never work in nursing again?"

It was a fair question. Cam knew that, while Jo Ella was a dedicated and highly efficient nurse, she had not gone into the profession for any of the usual noble reasons. She hated pain and she hated suffering; an athletic and determinedly healthy young woman herself, she waged her own private war against the infirmities that imprisoned the human body behind hospital walls. That was the passion that made her a good nurse. But the practicality of it was that the profession offered her freedom: good pay, endless job openings, variety. She could work for six months at one hospital and three months as a private-duty nurse for some rich old man and eight months in a foreign clinic and never feel tied to one place because of finances or security. She could get a job in any city in the world with three days notice, and that, if one were to be brutally blunt, was why Jo

Ella had chosen that career. For the freedom. But now the open walls had turned into prison cells, and Cam did not think she would have much trouble making the decision to get out.

For just one brief moment, Jo Ella's mind was filled with the sight of Bobby Williams, a twenty-three-year-old, a college football star, his body shrunken and wasted on the hospital bed, his face twisted with pain. It was a flash that came to her at unexpected times, and she supposed it always would. She did not know whether or not she would ever learn to live with it. But at least Cam had not said the one word that could have sent her over the edge, and Jo Ella loved him for that. Euthanasia—an ugly, harsh and cold word, the sound and the sight of which haunted her for eight long months. But it was better than the other word. Murder.

Cameron saw the dark veil obscure her troubled eyes, and then he saw her push it away with her familiar resilience of spirit. She said, "I don't know, Cam." Her voice was quiet. "It's beginning to look as though I don't have much choice."

He nodded once, decisively. "So what are you going to do?"

Again her answer was a sigh. "I don't know. Look for something else, I suppose."

Cameron could not prevent a small, troubled frown from darkening his features. This did not sound like Jo Ella. The listlessness, the indecision, the . . . hopelessness. She was entitled, he supposed, after what she had been through, but still it worried him.

She squared her shoulders, and the energy it seemed to cost her looked to be her last. "Whatever I do, it had better be quick," she said. "Mom lent me the money for this trip, and it's about gone. I can't afford to stay more than a couple of days."

He nodded, still watching her. "Well, here you are in the biggest city in Texas, opportunity knocking on every door; you can't afford to be out to lunch when it finally hits yours."

Jo Ella laughed a little, somewhat falsely. She drained the last of her iced tea. "From the mouth of the prophet."

Cam simply sat there, watching her, and for some unknown reason his steady gaze made Jo Ella nervous. She had never felt nervous with Cam before. But then, she was feeling a lot of things these days she had never felt before. That was why she hadn't called him.

What was he thinking? Was he looking into her soul, making his own assessments of her guilt or innocence? Was he examining her capabilities, was he letting that demon of suspicion invade the sanctity of their relationship? Oh, please, not Cam. She couldn't bear it if Cam turned against her, if she looked up and saw that opaque screen of carefully hidden revulsion in Cam's eyes. That was why she hadn't called him.

"You know what I think?" Cam said abruptly, startling her. She raised her eyes to his almost fearfully, but if he noticed her unusual reaction to the sound of his voice he gave no indication of it. "You're shell-shocked. Battle fatigue. What you need right now is a chance to rest and get yourself back together."

"Oh, Cam," Jo Ella said with a tired smile. "That's all I've been doing for the past eight months. Being pampered and babied and smothered to death...."

And she shook her head slowly. "I just don't know how I can go back to that." There was a quiet desperation in her voice that she tried unsuccessfully to hide. "Mom meant well, Cam, but—the walls were closing in on me. I can't go back there, I can't go on like that."

"Nobody said you had to," he agreed equitably. "Like I said, you can't afford to be that far away from opportunity. You need to stay in Dallas."

She made a small hopeless sound. "Don't I wish."

He lifted his eyebrows in a mild challenge. "So why don't you?"

"No job, no money, no place to stay," Jo Ella explained with uncharacteristic patience. "Simple facts of life."

"So stay with me until you get on your feet again. No problem."

The offer came at the same moment Jo Ella's eyes had dropped to the table and rested on his hand. That lean, rough, mechanic's hand that had once played like music over her body and taught her about life and loving and womanhood, the slender fingers that had brought her to an awareness of senses she had not even known she possessed...for a moment all she could do was look at his hand, and it took a long time for the words to sink in.

She looked up at him slowly. Was he remembering? There was no sign of it on his face. And why should there be? It was all so long ago. They had tried and failed, for one brief moment they had held something beautiful in their hands, but it was gone now. Part of the past.

She recovered herself enough to say automatically, "That's very generous of you, Cam."

He shrugged it off. "Don't say 'generous' until you've seen my place. It's no Taj Mahal, but there's room. You can fly down tomorrow and pick up the rest of your things and move in tomorrow night. No big deal."

Jo Ella stared at him. Cam was a man of quick and precise decisions. She had forgotten that about him. "Wait a minute, I can't afford to fly—"

"Nobody said anything about money. Burt has to take a couple of cattlemen down to Lubbock tomorrow morning—he was going to stop by and see your mom anyway. You can ride in the cargo hold."

Her head was spinning, and she missed Cam's attempt at humor. Why not, she kept thinking. She needed to stay here, she needed a chance to look for a job, she desperately needed to get away from home... she needed a friend. Why not? She would have done the same for Cam if he was in trouble. He wouldn't have volunteered if he hadn't meant it; Cam was simply not that generous. And it wouldn't be for long, just until she got settled.... Why not? She couldn't think of a single reason why not.

"Cam, I can't impose...." She began feebly, and he only looked annoyed. "I can't just pack up and move—"

"Sure you can. Just throw your clothes in a suitcase. It's all settled." He picked up the check. "You just meet Burt at the airfield about eight in the morning—he'll be looking for you."

Cameron was also positively intractable once his mind was made up. That was another thing Jo Ella had forgotten about him.

"Cam, I don't know. . . ." She felt certain there were a dozen very good reasons why this was a bad idea, and how long had it been since she had made an impulsive decision—the kind she was renowned for? The old Jo Ella wouldn't have hesitated a minute. The old Jo Ella never looked before she leaped. But the past year had brought caution and fear and worry, and Jo Ella was appalled to realize how much of herself she had lost.

Cameron stood up, waiting for her, and Jo Ella looked up at him in one last moment of helpless indecision. Then he smiled at her and extended his hand. After only another second of hesitation, Jo Ella put her own hand in it.

It was as simple as that.

Chapter Three

Jo Ella was still having difficulty believing what she had committed herself to do when Cam came to help her check out of the motel the next morning. Her one suitcase was tossed lightly into the back seat of his car, to be delivered to his apartment later, and they were on their way to the airfield before eight o'clock in the morning.

"I called your mother last night," Cam told her. "I knew you'd forget to. She's expecting you and Burt for lunch."

Jo Ella shot him a brief, grateful look that was only slightly underscored with anxiety. Wonderful Cam, always taking care of everything. But... "Did you tell her"—she could not quite keep a note of hopefulness from creeping into her voice—"why I was moving to Dallas? That I was moving in with you?"

Cam's returned gaze was tolerant and understanding. "That's one you're going to have to handle on your own, little bird. I just made the appointment for you."

Jo Ella sighed. It would have been nice to have been spared the scene with her mother, but she should have known Cam's helpfulness would stop short of interference.

She was still certain she was doing the right thing. It would be impractical, not to mention agonizing, to stay in Lubbock any longer. She had to find work, and the best place to do that was in Dallas. For her own mental health she needed to get away from the small town with its smothering memories of the past year, to escape from the stigma that had been attached to her and fade into anonymity. She needed a chance to start over again. Moving in with Cam was a heaven-sent opportunity, and one she simply couldn't afford to turn down.

She only hoped her mother would see it that way.

Jo Ella hadn't seen Burt in almost five years, but he hadn't changed much. He was still confident, energetic, purposeful and just a little bit arrogant—in many ways the complementary opposite of his brother. He swept her off her feet with an exaggerated kiss, gave her a playful pat on the bottom, and welcomed her to Dallas. In the next breath he was on the phone with ground control, studying the flight charts, and before she knew it he had disappeared onto the airfield, presumably to begin the preflight check. Cam grinned at her, told her he would see her tonight, and gave her a casual wink before wandering back toward the hangar to begin his working day.

They were in the air within an hour.

It would have taken two days for Jo Ella to drive to Lubbock, collect her things and drive back, and she was grateful for the flight that would take less than two hours. She had not realized that, in addition to the helicopter charter that served Dallas–Fort Worth and the surrounding area, Burt also had an arrangement with a small plane outfit for longer excursions. The four-seater Cessna he flew was comfortable and efficient, and Jo Ella enjoyed the trip from the copilot's seat next to Burt.

Burt himself went out of his way to be an amiable companion, but then, being charming was one of Burt's favorite things to do. His two passengers were busily absorbed in the back with their briefcases and their business strategy, and Burt devoted his full attention to Jo Ella. He brought her up to date on the progress of the business—which, Jo Ella knew from infrequent conversations with Cam over the years, was thriving—he teased her with reminiscences of their childhood, and he even let her take over the controls for a few minutes. He never once mentioned the scandal of the past year of Jo Ella's life, and for that she was more than grateful.

"You could have made a pilot, you know that?" Burt took the controls back from her with a grin as they prepared for the initial approach into Lubbock. "You've got the instinct for it."

Jo Ella laughed. She had begged Burt to take her up every time she saw him since the first day he had gotten his pilot's license; every time he pretended reluctance—and always capitulated—and every time he ended up giving her a mini flying lesson. And every time he made the same comment. "Maybe next lifetime," she answered him, focusing her attention on the flat brown landscape below them. It was so vast, so endless; she reveled in it. Jo Ella had always said the best thing about flying was the view from the sky.

Burt cast her a single shrewd look. "Yeah, you're a pretty busy lady."

Jo Ella tensed then, expecting the observation to lead to a discussion of her recent activities, but she should have known Burt would never make a point of putting her in an uncomfortable position. He was Cam's brother, after all.

"So," he said merely, "Cam tells me you'll be staying in Dallas for a while."

She assumed accurately that Cam had also told Burt the details of her future living arrangement, for she saw no reason why he would keep it a secret from his brother. Still, she watched Burt's face carefully as she replied, "Cam said I could stay with him until I got settled."

Burt kept his face carefully neutral as he nodded. "I don't suppose you have any idea how long that will be?"

It was an innocent comment, or it should have been. There was nothing in his tone or his expression to put Jo Ella on the defensive, but still she got the very strong impression that Burt did not approve. And she turned her eyes back to the window as she answered, "No, not really. Just until I can find a job."

"It'll be nice having you around." The statement sounded more polite than genuine, and very unlike Burt. "Just like old times."

"Old times." Was there a double meaning to that phrase, or was Jo Ella simply imagining it? Was he referring to the carefree days of their youth when the three of them were inseparable, or to more recent time, when it was Jo Ella and Cam who were never seen without each other? Burt's face was bland, and it would be ridiculous to read either a warning or a reprimand there, but Jo Ella for some reason felt compelled to insist that it wasn't like old times at all, that the living arrangement was only for convenience, that her relationship with Cam was purely platonic, that he was nothing more than an old friend doing her a favor. But she said nothing. Perhaps it was because she wasn't entirely sure how true her denials were, or how true she wanted them to be.

At any rate, Burt did not give her a chance. He switched on the microphone for landing instructions, and the subject was not brought up again.

Burt treated her like a first-class paying passenger. He had a car waiting to drive her to her mother's house and told her he had some things to follow up on in town and would meet her there at noon. When Jo Ella began to thank him effusively for all his trouble, he merely waved it away with a grin, saying, "Are you kidding? One of your mom's home-cooked meals is more than worth the fare. As a matter of fact," he added, "I have you to thank for two home-cooked meals today. My mom wants us all for dinner tonight."

Jo Ella kept her smile cheerful, but inwardly she winced. An afternoon spent with her mother would more than fill her tolerance for family gatherings, and she had really looked forward to some peace and quiet later on.

The square yellow house sat baking in the sun at the end of a dusty dirt road, just as Jo Ella had left it less than a week ago. Her mother was sitting in the morning shade of the front porch, snapping beans for dinner. Jo

Ella greeted her with a kiss and sat down beside her, scooping up a handful of beans from the bucket at her feet.

"Put an apron on, Jo Ella," Lilly Cable advised. "You're going to stain your slacks."

Jo Ella began methodically to break the beans into fourths, dropping the discarded ends into the sack on the floor, tossing the broken beans into the pot on her mother's lap. "Cam sends his love, and Burt's looking forward to one of your home-cooked meals," she said, by way of leading up to the subject of her decision to stay in Dallas.

Lilly chuckled, nodding approvingly. "Good boys, both of them. Not that they should be hungering for home cooking, with their mother living just down the street."

Lilly could never get it through her head that Dallas was not just another small hometown where everyone knew everyone else, and where every street was within walking distance of the next. Jo Ella knew that it was almost an hour's drive from Cam's apartment to his mother's house, and she doubted that he made it over there every night for dinner. But there was no sense in trying to tell Lilly that.

"How is Avis, anyway?" Lilly inquired.

By the same token, Lilly could not imagine that Jo Ella had been in Dallas two days and had not run into Avis Scott on the street. Jo Ella wondered what her mother would say if she knew that, in fact, it had been Cam who called her, and not the other way around. She still was not sure if she might have left town without ever seeing any of them, had not Cam made the first move.

"Fine, I guess," Jo Ella replied absently, dumping more snapped beans into the pot. "We're all going there for dinner tonight."

Again Lilly nodded, with enthusiasm and approval. "Well, tell me about your job. I started putting some of your things together—had to drag down an old suitcase from the attic. What did you do with your suitcases, Jo?" She looked at her daughter curiously. "I looked everywhere for them." Then she shrugged it away. "We'll find them later. Now, the job. Why didn't you call me? I want to hear all about it, every word."

Jo Ella felt herself start to wither inside. This was not going to be easy. Not at all. "Mom," she began with difficulty, placing the last of the beans in the pot. "I don't exactly have a job...."

Lilly raised a curious eyebrow. "But I thought Cam said— I didn't misunderstand, did I? You are flying back to Dallas this afternoon, aren't you?" She shook her head in exasperation. "Long distance is so frustrating. I never can catch but half of what the other person is saying, and Cam's not the most talkative person in the world, anyway. You would think that after calling all this way he'd want to chat awhile, but he couldn't have been on the phone for more than a minute." She looked at Jo Ella alertly. "He's not having money problems, do you think? I would have paid for the call...."

Jo Ella could not prevent a touch of amusement from showing in her face as she shook her head tiredly. Her mother's conversations were exhausting, being, for the most part, one sided. Jo Ella admired Cam for being able to keep the call under a minute. Only he could get away with it.

"No, Mom, Cam's doing just fine. As a matter of fact"—she lowered her eyes and busied herself with brushing the small green remnants of beans off her slacks—"he's offered me a place to stay while I'm in Dallas, looking for work."

Lilly's attention sharpened. "Do you mean you're moving to Dallas and you don't even have a job? Jo Ella, dear, do you think that's wise? I mean, the way things are now, who knows how long you could be out of work, or what you'll even be able to find. We've talked about this before. And while I'm sure it's very nice of the Scotts to offer you a place to stay, you certainly can't impose forever. Now, I've talked to Mr. Goss down at the five-and-dime, and he says he'll be glad to take you on part-time. I know it's not much, but..."

Jo Ella felt herself sinking, slowly, inexorably, drowning in the tide of her mother's good intentions. And, in a fierce self-protective mechanism, she began to shake her head firmly. "No," she said, quite a bit more sharply than she had intended. Her mother looked startled. "No. No five-and-dimes, no insurance offices, no civil service..." She gentled her voice with an effort. "Mom, I told you before I left—I can't find work in Lubbock. I'm a career woman, I have to have a *real* job, one that pays enough to live on."

"You always have a place to live with me," replied Lilly, hurt.

Jo Ella sighed. It was always like this with her mother. Everything she did or said made her feel guilty...and trapped. "I know, Mom," she said. "It's not that, it's just that I need to be independent, you know?"

Lilly released a long-suffering breath. "I suppose if I haven't learned that in almost thirty years, I never will." And, resigned, she added, "Well, all things considered, you could do a sight worse than Dallas, I suppose. I know I'll feel a lot better knowing you're with Avis than if you were out in some jungle or off on the high seas or something.

Jo Ella took a breath. "Mom..." She couldn't put it off any longer. "I won't be living with Avis. I'll be staying with Cam."

Although Lilly Cable should have been immune to her daughter's surprises by now, for that first brief moment she couldn't hide her shock—or her disapproval. "Cameron?" she echoed. "Do you mean—alone with him, in his apartment?"

Jo Ella tried to smile; the result was a little strained. "Yes, alone with him, in his apartment—and you needn't make it sound like Sodom and Gomorrah."

"Well, I'm sure I never..." Flustered, Lilly began to make futile motions that pretended to arrange the beans in the pot, dust off her apron and sweep a strand of hair behind her ear. "I just never realized..."

Jo Ella's irritation was rising, and there was no good reason for it. Her mother was trying very hard to be mature about this, but the things she was not saying were ringing louder in Jo Ella's ears than a tirade of accusations could have done.

"It's nothing like that, Mom." Jo Ella made her voice very, very patient. "Cam's just being a good friend, that's all. He has the room, and I need a place to stay. We're both mature adults."

Lilly fastened her with a meaningful look. "Exactly." And then, somewhat helplessly, "Well, you always were a headstrong little thing, and nothing I can say will change your mind, I know." She began to gather up the pots of beans. "I just don't know what the minister is going to say...."

Her voice trailed off as she went inside, the screen door bouncing lightly behind her. It resumed again from somewhere within the depths of the house. "After all that's happened this past year, it looks as though you'd be ready to settle down and have a nice, quiet life for a while. Jo Ella, are you coming in?"

Jo Ella could feel tension nagging at the back of her neck like a giant claw. The lecture, carefully disguised as a discussion and an offer of helpful advice, would continue until Burt arrived, and Jo Ella did not think she could take that. She was suddenly consumed by an urge to run, to just get up and sprint across the open fields with the wind in her hair and the sun in her face, inhaling the scent of dry Texas soil and clean, unfettered air.

"In a minute, Mom," she called back. "I'm going to get my suitcases out of the barn first."

And then she did run, bouncing down the steps two at a time, covering the ground between house and barn with long, muscle-driven strides. The short distance barely winded her, but she arrived at the barn feeling somewhat purged and much calmer for the exercise.

Though Lilly did not use the barn or work the acres herself, she rented out most of the land for alfalfa and the barn for storage. Bales of sweet-smelling hay filled the loft and most of the lower portion, and Jo Ella stood there for a moment, inhaling the fragrance and watching the way shafts of sunshine sliced across the musky interior, catching motes of dust and illuminating them for a moment like an aimless collection of wayward thoughts.

This had always been a peaceful place for Jo Ella, the storehouse for all her favorite childhood memories. They had all played here as children, and the barn had taken its turn as an ancient castle or a manor house or a World War II bunker, or the flight tower of an international airport. And as they grew older...

Her suitcases were as she had left them, in a corner reserved for personal storage between the stacked bales of hay. She had covered them with an old army blanket, the same one that had been hanging from a bent nail inside the barn for as long as she could remember—and the same one she and Cam had lain upon that rainy spring afternoon so many years ago. She made her way over to it, lifting the corner and bringing its scratchy texture to her cheek, rubbing it against her skin thoughtfully. She stood there for a moment, remembering.

IT WAS THE WEEKEND Avis was moving to Dallas. Burt and Cam had driven a big U-Haul down, and Jo Ella, who was living in Dallas at the time while she completed her internship at a large midtown hospital, had somehow been volunteered to help. Two of Jo Ella's sisters were living in town at the time, her eldest brother was home for a visit, complete with wife and children, and the normal amount of chaos at Sunday dinner at Lilly Cable's house was compounded by Avis's tearful goodbyes and uncertainty about moving.

Jo Ella's well-meaning relatives, filled with good advice, were in their element that weekend, for there was not only Avis's life to be settled, but Jo Ella's as well. Her mother wanted Jo Ella to come back home and apply for a position in a local hospital. Her brother informed her that there was no money in nursing and she was crazy to have spent all that time and effort on education. She should have gone into computers. One sister replied that it hardly mattered, since Jo Ella would surely be getting married before too much longer and there was hardly a better place to find an eligible doctor than in a hospital. The other sister, now six glorious months pregnant, insisted that what Jo Ella should really do was to check out the new program for nurse-midwives. She could end up running her own clinic.

After a while it started to rain, and the clamorous sound of five conversations going at once mingled to an almost deafening level with the scattering of rain on the roof. Lilly closed the windows, and the air inside the room became hot and close, hard to breathe. Jo Ella felt that smothering sense of claustrophobia creeping up on her, and she couldn't stay another minute. On the pretense of refilling her iced-tea glass, she slipped out the kitchen door and sprinted across the muddy yard to the shelter of the barn.

It was cool there, rain-washed and hay-fresh. The pinging of rain on the metal barn roof was cheerful and light, reminding her of open spaces and miles and miles of slanting rain watering a thirsty desert. There was a nest of birds in the loft, and their low shrilling was a musical counterpoint to the sound of the gentle storm. Jo Ella let the tension be carried away by the breeze as she pulled down the old blanket, dried her hair with it, and wrapped it around her damp shoulders. She sank to the floor with the wall as a backrest, and relaxed to the sound and the smells of the rain, the perfect peace of her own refuge from the storm.

She tensed when a shadow appeared at the door; relaxed again when she saw it was only Cam. She laughed as he shook the rain out of his hair and futilely brushed at his shirt, which was already soaked. "Got to you, too, did they?" she teased, and he grinned.

"Let's just say I felt in the mood for a game of hide-and-seek." And he shivered, shaking his wet hair again. "That rain is cold."

Jo Ella lifted a corner of the blanket, offering him half, and he sank down beside her, using the edge of the blanket to wipe his face and neck before draping it negligently over part of his shoulders.

It seemed the moment was predestined. Perhaps, subconsciously, both of them had had a part in planning it. Because when they looked at each other and smiled, there was no doubt in either mind as to how this interlude in the barn would eventually end.

Jo Ella had been interning in Dallas for two months, and she had seen a great deal of Cam during that time. It was only natural—one old friend making another feel at home in a strange city. Whenever their paths crossed, they spent most of their time together until something happened to separate them again—Cam's Coast Guard duty, Jo Ella's school, Cam's new business—but this time they were in the same place at the same time and it was more than just two old friends passing time together. They both knew it.

As teenagers, Jo Ella had been aware that Cam was the best-looking boy in school; all the girls were after him. She had not thought much about it. She had her own boyfriends, and Cam was just—Cam. When she was thirteen and Cam was sixteen, Cam had kissed her; it was the first time any boy had kissed her on the lips. At thirteen, Jo Ella had just graduated from Barbie dolls and still had occasional lapses into the tree-climbing stage; she was not very impressed, and the entire experience seemed to embarrass Cam. By the time Jo Ella was ready to experiment with the intricacies of boy-girl behavior, Cam was no longer interested, and besides, there were plenty of other candidates crowding the doorstep of one of the most popular girls in school. As teenagers, she and Cam went out together for fun; they never "dated" each other.

The first time Jo Ella had seen Cam in his Coast Guard uniform, she had been shocked by what a devastatingly good-looking man he was. She was fairly experienced by then, and she understood exactly why the girls were always after him in high school. But after that first brief insight, Cam was once again just Cam, her friend and confidant, and the brief times they spent together were no different than they had ever been. Besides, Cam was dating someone else, and Jo Ella was soon due to return to college, where she had a boyfriend waiting.

It was not until this very spring that Jo Ella had actually thought of Cam as a sexual being. Having thought of it, she could not get it off her mind. And she knew he felt the same way about her.

When she first moved to Dallas, Cam had spent a lot of time helping her get settled in, showing her around town, taking her out to dinner. Those were the normal things a friend would do for another. But later, the times they spent together were more like dates. It had happened so gradually Jo Ella did not know what had made the difference, but she knew there was a difference.

He had never even kissed her—not since that first time at age thirteen—but he wanted to. It was in the way he looked at her. And the way he touched her. There had always been an easy demonstration of affection between Cam and Jo Ella—neither were shy about touching—but there was a new meaning to the gestures they shared now. A gentle holding of hands, a caress of the face, a touch of the hair, arms around each other's waists or hands resting lightly on each other's knees—there was a subtle undercurrent of awareness to each movement now that neither could ignore, nor did they want to. That was why, as Jo Ella snuggled into the crook of his arm that afternoon beneath the folds of the damp-smelling blanket, she felt as though something wonderful and long awaited was about to happen. And anticipation made her heart beat faster.

Cam's eyes crinkled as he looked down at her. There were still drops of moisture clinging to his forehead. "Remember when we used to make a tent out here and pretend we were foot soldiers on patrol? This isn't the same blanket, is it?"

Jo Ella laughed. "I'm afraid so." She sniffed the

folds of the blanket delicately. "No too much the worse for wear. Funny how it smells like horses though we never had a horse in here in our lives."

Cam's arm slid down to rest comfortably around her waist. His fingers were warm through the thin wet material of her shirt, and he smelled like sunshine. Sunshine on a rainy day. "I remember when you tried to get your dad to buy you a colt to raise for 4-H," Cam said with a chuckle. "He was not very amused."

"He said if the rest of the family could get along on pigs for projects, I shouldn't be any different. One thing about Dad, he didn't show any favoritism for the youngest."

"Despite your best efforts," Cam reminded her.

They settled against each other, his arm around her waist, her hand entwined comfortably with his and holding it against her thigh, and for a time they listened to the sound of the rain and the twitter of the nest of birds, warming each other through their damp clothes. And as they sat, awareness of him began to tighten like a secret in the pit of Jo Ella's stomach, tingling in her pulse and glowing in her skin. It was wonderful to be with him like that. More than wonderful.

She looked up at him. There was shyness in her eyes, but she felt bold. And she could feel the boldness heightening the color of her cheeks, deepening the sparkle in her eyes. "Do you remember," she said, "the time I asked you to teach me to French-kiss?"

Cam laughed a little, but it sounded somewhat strained. He pushed a wet strand of hair behind her ear. His eyes seemed to be busy trying to look into her soul. "I sure do. It's probably one of the most unnerving things that ever happened to me." Cam's fingers lingered against her face, gently separating a tangle at her temple. His eyes were absorbed in the task.

"You told me I was too young."

"You were."

"I was fifteen!" she asserted.

"And I," Cam reminded her gently, "was eighteen." There was soberness in his eyes even as he smiled. "Not the time of life a young man wants to be locked away for molesting a minor." His fingers began to trail down her face, tracing the outline of her jaw, brushing, just barely, against her lips. She could feel the quickening of her breath with his touch, and she thought she sensed a similar response in him.

"Would you?" she asked, somewhat breathlessly. "Would you have...have..."

She did not finish, and Cam did not answer. His eyes were dark and enigmatic, and when his fingers began to play gently across her collarbone, Jo Ella forgot what she had wanted to ask. She merely whispered, "Am I still too young, Cam?"

Very slowly, very carefully, he brought his hand to her face again. His eyes held her, and caressed her, and signaled every move before he made it. His forefinger touched her lips lightly, parting them. And he brought his open mouth down to cover hers.

Jo Ella embraced sex as she did everything else in life, with enthusiasm and verve. It had always been for her a pleasurable activity, physically satisfying, nicely relaxing...fun. If there was anything missing—an emotional emptiness, a mental frustration—she had never noticed it before. Until that afternoon with Cam, and she discovered for the very first time that there was something more.

Perhaps it was her naturally aggressive personality, or perhaps it was merely her choice of partners, but Jo Ella had grown accustomed to being in charge in the bedroom. She approached the act of physical intimacy with her usual energetic confidence, a goal to be conquered, a prize to be won, and a moment of rest before she moved on. She had little patience with foreplay or amenities. Cam, that afternoon, taught her differently.

Gently and patiently, he took control. He set the pace, he refused to be rushed. And with his usual care and cautious deliberation, he showed her dimensions of pleasure she had never before imagined were possible.

In all the years she had known Cam, she had never fantasized about what he would be like as a lover. Even recently, when she had begun to see him differently, she had known only that she wanted to make love with him; she had known only that, because it was Cam, it would be wonderful.

And it was wonderful. Never before had a single kiss aroused her to such a level. The touch of his fingers, and then his lips, on her breasts was an excruciating agony of yearning. Her hands began to fumble with his clothing, urging him impatiently toward fulfillment, but he merely smiled and shifted away, turning his attention to the curve of her neck and the hollow of her ear, and every nibbling kiss, every brushing caress, brought her to a new level of urgent excitement, magnifying pleasure in a thousand unexpected ways.

When he undressed her it was only to allow his hands and his lips to discover every inch of flesh he exposed. It was beautiful, endless, agonizing. And when he removed his own clothes and drew her gently against him, the sensation of his body, full and naked, against hers, was dizzying and powerful. Not since the changes in their bodies had put an end to days of skinny-dipping had Jo Ella seen Cam naked. He was strong, lean and intensely masculine. Even the sight of him took her breath away. And for a long time he simply held her, his large body sheltering and enfolding hers. For years afterward Jo Ella would remember above all else the way it had felt to be held naked against Cam.

The moment of consummation was as tender and as beautiful as all that had led up to it. He entered her with careful, agonizing slowness, allowing her aching flesh time to adjust to his size, to absorb him and welcome him. And all the while he kissed her, while he stroked her face and her hair in soothing, gently repetitive motions, he smiled at her. That smile—the warm, wonderful affection in his eyes—was the most beautiful thing Jo Ella had ever seen. It, too, would haunt her for years.

Making love with Cam was a physical act turned into something magical. It was the warmth and comfort of two people who knew each other so well they could anticipate needs before they were voiced, it was the unexpected excitement of something familiar turned abruptly new; it was, for Jo Ella, the very first time she had made love with a person and not just a body. It was the most wonderful thing that had ever happened to her, and it left her so overwhelmed she could not even absorb it.

Afterward they lay curled up together with one corner of the blanket pulled over them for warmth, touching each other, holding each other. Usually Jo Ella lost interest after satisfaction; she wanted to sleep or eat or sit up and talk. But now she wanted nothing more than to touch Cam, to hold him and feel him holding her, to marvel over what they had just shared.

Cam's breath fluttered across her cheek, his hands tightened on her waist, pressing her briefly closer. "Ah, Joey." He sighed. "Why did we wait so long?"

Jo Ella didn't know. It was all so new to her. She simply couldn't absorb, at that moment, how special it really was.

Perhaps the biggest mistake of her life had been that she had never really appreciated how special it was. Not until it was too late.

"Jo Ella?" Her mother's voice jarred Jo Ella out of her reverie. "Did you find them?"

Jo Ella tossed aside the blanket and bent to lift her suitcases. "Yeah, Mom," she called back. "I'm coming."

"I could use some help in the kitchen."

"Coming!" Joey reiterated, louder, so that her voice would carry.

With a suitcase in each hand, Jo Ella squared her shoulders and started back toward the house, ready to face an afternoon of motherly advice and silent recriminations.

But part of her mind, perhaps the largest part, was still back with Cam and the three months of a love-drenched spring and summer they had shared so long ago. She was wondering how it had slipped away so easily.

She was wondering if anything remained of it now.

Chapter Four

All in all, it wasn't as bad as it could have been. Jo Ella's mother wouldn't have dreamed of making a scene in front of Burt and, in fact, had long since learned that going up against Jo Ella on any issue was a waste of time. She resigned herself to the inevitable and tried to hide her disapproval, but it was obvious she did not want her daughter to leave.

Jo Ella could not relate to that. She had lived with her mother ever since she had lost her job, she had placed an enormous emotional and financial burden on her, they had done nothing but get in each other's way and on each other's nerves. Why wasn't Lilly as glad to have her own life back as Jo Ella was to have hers? Jo Ella had little patience with her mother's suffering. The very walls of the house seemed to breathe the stale scent of guilt and accusation and of things left too long locked inside, and Jo Ella could not wait to get out. She knew at that moment that, whatever happened, she would not regret moving in with Cam. It would probably save her sanity.

Burt, always the sociable type, wanted to spend the

afternoon visiting, so Jo Ella took her time about packing. Burt and her mother sat on the front porch, sipping lemonade and catching up on all the gossip from both sides, while Jo Ella methodically emptied the contents of her drawers and closet into two compact suitcases. She did not have much. Jo Ella was accustomed to wearing uniforms, and besides, she believed in traveling light.

Cam was just closing down the shop when they touched down at the Dallas–Fort Worth airport. He was wearing greasy coveralls, and a sweaty red bandanna kept his hair from flopping down over his face, which was also rather greasy. He greeted his brother and Jo Ella with a grin and a casual wave, then went to shower and change—just as though this happened to him every day of his life.

They loaded Jo Ella's suitcases into the trunk of Cam's Grand Prix, then Burt climbed into his Camaro and they split up to reunite for the dinner at their mother's house. Jo Ella was struck, not for the first time, by the difference in the two brothers. Cameron drove a car that would have been better suited to an old man; Burt, the family man, drove a sports car for all it was worth. Burt flew the planes, Cam worked on them. They made a perfect team, she supposed.

"Better get it over with now," Cam confided to Jo Ella when they were under way, "or she'll be pestering us until we do."

Jo Ella smiled, trying not to let him know how much she dreaded another family scene. "I could have stayed with your mother," she volunteered, but it was not the first time she had thought of it. She only felt it was fair to give him his options. "Or with Burt and Mary. You didn't have to put yourself out—"

"Ma would drive you crazy," he answered. "And Burt and Mary don't have the room. Besides, none of them asked you." And he glanced at her with a wicked little twinkle in his eye. "Not worried about your reputation, are you?"

Jo Ella gave a little snort of laughter. "Hardly!" No, that was not what she was worried about. Not at all.

But as soon as they pulled into the short driveway of Avis Scott's small ranch-style house, Jo Ella did not have time to worry about anything anymore. Three noisy T-shirted boys ranging in age from three to seven ran to meet them, totally ignoring their father, who was just climbing out of his Camaro, for the rarer treat of their uncle. Jo Ella winced through her laughter as Cam's freshly laundered shirt quickly became smudged by grubby hands, bubble-gum-covered faces lifted to his for a kiss, a muddy football bounced off his shin, and a cup of grape juice was spilled on his arm. And Cam seemed to love it. He retrieved the football and sent the oldest boy out for a pass, placated the other two with a pack of gum wisely stored in his pocket for just such emergencies, stripped off his shirt and tossed it to his mother for laundering. Then he sprinted across the lawn and wrestled the oldest boy for possession of the football, and the game was on.

Mary, eight months pregnant and looking every minute of it, embraced Jo Ella like a long-lost friend, even though the two women had only met on one or two occasions. Avis looked Jo Ella over once, shrewdly, pronounced that she was badly in need of fattening up, and ushered both women into the house to help prepare dinner.

This was only an echo of the grand chaos that had pervaded Jo Ella's childhood—the noise, the clutter, little feet running in and out, the television set blaring the evening news from the other room, a steamy kitchen filled with good smells and women moving with assembly-line efficiency from stove to refrigerator to dining room while never missing a beat in the unending chatter about children and husbands—their own and everyone else's. It should have made Jo Ella nostalgic, or amused at the very least, but in fact it only made her a little breathless. She had never handled crowds very well.

When there was nothing to be done but wait for the homemade rolls to brown and Avis and Mary were deep in conversation about Mary's three-year-old's bed-wetting problem, Jo Ella felt it was safe to slip outside for a moment. The patio overlooked a handkerchief-sized backyard and three houses whose walls came within inches of forming a perfect box around Avis's house. It amazed Jo Ella that in this highly priced residential area, with all the thousands of unused acres around the Dallas–Fort Worth area, houses should be built so closely together that a full-sized person could barely squeeze between them. It was that way all over Texas. You could drive for miles and see nothing but open space, and when you finally came upon a residential area, the houses would be so crowded that you could shake hands with your neighbor from your bedroom window. What happened to the land of open spaces? Was Jo Ella Cable the only person in the world who needed freedom to breathe?

She could see the football game still in noisy progress in the front yard, and she walked to the edge of the patio for a better view. She wondered if Cam had any idea how sexy he looked with his shirt off. His chest was smooth and brown, now lightly oiled with perspiration, his waist spare and abdomen flat above the low-slung jeans. The setting sun rippled off flexing shoulder muscles as he leaned back for a pass, and Jo Ella's eyes focused for some reason on the light tangle of hair beneath his upraised arm. And watching him surprised a sensation deep within her abdomen—a startled recognition, an almost forgotten memory, something she had not felt in years. And she quickly choked it off and turned away before her questing mind could analyze it.

The patio door slid open, and Jo Ella smiled automatically as Mary came out. Mary might once have been a pretty girl, with her curly black hair and large gray eyes; nine years of marriage and three and a half children later, she looked only tired. She sank down on one of the webbed chairs on the patio, sprawling with her knees apart and her abdomen taking the center of gravity, and looked up at Jo Ella with a smile. "Cam says you'll be staying with him for a while. That's nice. He doesn't live too far from us, you know. We can have lunch sometimes."

Jo Ella could not imagine herself enjoying a lunch with three active boys and a pregnant lady. Things were depressing enough as they were. But she responded easily, "Sure, that sounds good. But my first priority is to get a job."

Mary's eyes lit up with what could only be described as envy. "Cam said you worked on a cruise ship."

Jo Ella nodded. "That was a few years back. I've had a dozen or so jobs since then." Including one in an Austin hospital where she had met a young man by the name of Bobby Williams and never guessed he would change her life.

"But it sounds so glamorous!" Mary's eyes, caught for a moment in the dream, reflected the beautiful young woman she must once have been. "How could you bear to give it up?"

Jo Ella's smile was wry. "A ship—even a luxury liner—can get pretty small after six months. I started to feel closed in."

Mary made a pretense of understanding, though it was obvious she did not. "That's right. Cam said you never liked to stay in one place for very long. You're lucky, to have traveled as much as you have—seen so many different places and met so many different people."

Jo Ella nodded slowly. That was the one thing she had always liked about her life, it was true. Endless opportunity, constant new horizons, always places to go and things to do and a challenge around every corner. But... Her smile was a little sad as she spread her hands hopelessly. "I don't have too much to show for it," she said.

Mary's expression grew sober. "I want you to know, Jo Ella," she said quietly, "that none of us ever believed it. Not for a minute. We're all on your side."

Why should that simple sentiment, coming from an almost perfect stranger, bring a sting of tears to Jo Ella's eyes? The old family syndrome, she supposed. They would kill you with kindness.

Avis slid open the door and imperiously demanded their presence at the dinner table. Jo Ella blinked rapidly and even managed to share an amused look with Mary as they went inside.

Dinner was a zoo. It took fifteen minutes to get Cam and the boys cleaned up to the point that they met Avis's rather grudging approval, and that time was filled with screams and splashes and cries of agony from the bathroom as three adults confronted three children in a one-on-one over a bar of soap. Cam appeared at the table with his freshly laundered shirt—which was still damp around the collar and cuffs after only twenty minutes in the drier—unbuttoned to mid-chest and looking none the worse for wear, and Jo Ella was amazed. She was always a little in awe of people who could handle chaos without blinking an eye, and she had never realized Cam was so fond of children.

Avis was an excellent cook, so much so that Mary commented that no woman would ever have a chance of pleasing either of her two boys in the kitchen, they were so used to her standards of perfection. Burt grinned but did not contradict her. Jo Ella's enjoyment of the meal was somewhat impaired by the nonstop chatter, the demands for attention from the three boys, and her annoyance with Mary's persistence upon catering to the little despots. She was so busy cutting their meat, pouring their milk, refereeing food fights and persuading the three-year-old that his mashed potatoes were really ice cream that by the time Avis brought on a fluffy lemon meringue pie Mary's plate had hardly been touched. There were at least four conversations going on simultaneously, and Jo Ella's nerves grew frazzled with trying to keep up with them all. It was just like dinnertime at her own house, ten years ago.

The boys wolfed their pie and were sent out to play, and when only the adults remained Mary began to clear the table. Cam announced casually to his mother that Jo Ella was moving in with him tonight, and Jo Ella quickly decided to help Mary.

Avis gave Jo Ella another long, scrutinizing look, and Jo Ella's eyes, as she removed Cam's plate, could have killed. She did not mind breaking a few rules, but in front of his *mother*, for goodness' sake. It did appear to Jo Ella that this was one battle Cam could have fought with his mother before ever bringing Jo Ella on the scene, and she intended to make sure he knew it the moment they were alone. But Cam only returned a mildly amused glance at her discomfort, and Avis pronounced decisively, "You don't have enough linen."

She got up from the table in search of extra blankets, sheets and pillows, with Cam laughingly protesting all the while that it really wasn't necessary and Jo Ella staring after them both in openmouthed amazement. Avis Scott was, apparently, a law unto herself. There weren't too many mothers, after all, who, when her son announces he is living with a woman, would merely offer him an extra pillow.

It wasn't ten minutes later that Cam, armed with a stack of blankets, sheets, a pillow and three Tupperware containers of the leftovers from the night's feast balanced precariously on top of it all, began saying his goodbyes. Though Jo Ella was startled at this abrupt decision to depart, she was ashamed to admit she was also a little relieved, and did not argue when Cam gave as his excuse her fatigue after a long trip. She rescued the Tupperware as he bent to place the linen in the back seat, waved goodbye and thanked Avis for the meal, then climbed gratefully into the car.

Cam turned from forcing the pillow to lie flat on the seat just as Jo Ella straightened up from arranging the food containers on the floor; their eyes met, and they both burst into laughter.

Cam started the engine and reached a companionable hand across the seat to circle Jo Ella's neck. His eyes were still warm with laughter, and the pressure of his fingers on her taut neck muscles was wonderfully soothing. "You doing okay?" he inquired gently. "You were starting to look a little frazzled."

Jo Ella took a deep breath and nodded, letting the tension slide away from her now that the doors had closed on all the noise and people. "Your family is wonderful Cam, but—"

"A little claustrophobic at times," he agreed, and Jo Ella let herself sink into his understanding. She should have known there would be no need to explain to Cam.

The FM radio played a soothing melody on the long drive across town, and Cam did not talk. Jo Ella reveled in the silence, only then realizing how tired she really was. Her feet were throbbing and her back ached; her head felt as if it were stuffed with padded cotton. Culture shock, she thought to herself, the normal result of too many impulses hitting the brain at one time. It would take her a while to adjust.

Cam's apartment was small, but what else could she expect from a bachelor? At least it was on the top floor, and a balcony overlooked the lights of the city. Jo Ella knew she would spend a lot of time on that balcony.

Cam carried her suitcases in but had to make a second trip for the blankets and pillow. He refused her help, and Jo Ella used the time to get herself acquainted with the apartment.

The kitchen, where she went first to put away the food Cam's mother had packed up, was yellow, compact and sparsely stocked. The refrigerator contained a six-pack of beer and a carton of eggs. Apparently Cam had not inherited his mother's talent in the kitchen, and her gift of leftovers would be more than appreciated.

The living room–dining room combination was nicely furnished with a round oak table under a glass-globed chandelier and two matching bookcases flanking it. There was one large sofa and a love seat in a maroon print, a comfortable easy chair with a reading lamp, two hassocks and a wide, cushioned rocking chair. An aquarium bubbled on one wall, and an entertainment center covered the other. There were end tables with mismatched lamps, a coffee table and lots of throw cushions. It looked very... homey. As though Cam enjoyed living here.

There was only one bedroom. Cam had not told her that. Once again Jo Ella's mind went darting back to the spring of her twentieth year, and once again she pulled it forcefully back. But still she could not prevent a small knot of anxiety. Cam had not said or done, even indicated by a look or a meaningful silence, anything that would lead her to believe he was offering her anything except refuge from the storm for a short while. But why hadn't he told her about the sleeping arrangements? Was he setting her up for an awkward scene?

Jo Ella did not believe in postponing unpleasantness, and when Cam came back in she inquired directly, "Where am I going to sleep?"

He dumped the pillow and blanket on the armchair. "Didn't you find the bedroom?" He picked up two of her suitcases. "Here, it's this way."

Jo Ella hesitated, a look of uncertain distress crossing her face, and Cam met it patiently. "Sofa bed," he pointed out, shrugging one shoulder in that direction. "Plenty comfortable. I'll sleep there, you can have the bed, and we share the bathroom. Nothing could be simpler."

Two things bothered Jo Ella about that reply. First, it came so easily, as though no other possible arrangement had even crossed Cam's mind. They had been lovers once—good lovers, Jo Ella thought a little wistfully. Would it have been so odd if Cam had considered, even briefly, taking advantage of this situation to try to rekindle an old relationship? And the second thing was that this pragmatism was totally unlike Cam. She would have at least expected to be teased a little bit. Apparently he did not see their past as a basis for humor, and that disturbed Jo Ella.

At the door of his bedroom she stammered, "Cam, I—I can't put you out. I'll take the sofa bed."

He shrugged and lowered her suitcases to the floor. "Suit yourself. Right now"—he caught her hand and led her back into the living room—"you need to get off your feet. You can unpack in the morning." She sat down on the sofa, and he took both of her feet in one of his broad hands and swung them over the back of the sofa, forcing her to lie down. "Look at that," he said disparagingly as he pulled off her shoes. "You know your feet always swell when you fly. Your toes look like little fat sausages."

Jo Ella giggled and tucked a pillow beneath her head, moaning a little with pleasure as he began to massage her feet and ankles. "That feels wonderful, Cam," she murmured, letting her eyes close.

"No pounding the sidewalks for you tomorrow," he advised sternly, deft fingers working the circulation back into her feet. "My prescription is twenty-four hours of solid rest."

"I think I could go for that," she replied sleepily. It did feel so good to be off her feet. And it felt good not to worry about anything for a while. It felt safe here, in Cam's little second-story nest, protected and secure. For the first time she allowed herself to believe her troubles might really be behind her.

Cam sat beside her on the sofa, giving her upraised knees an impersonal pat, and Jo Ella opened her eyes with a smile to look at him. "Did I tell you how wonderful you are to do this for me?" she asked.

"It bears repeating if you have."

"You're wonderful to do this for me."

"Anytime."

His smile was as warm as sunshine, and the little crinkles around his eyes made Jo Ella want to reach out and touch them with her fingers. She had to tighten her hands to keep from doing so.

But it was Cam who moved his hand to stroke her

hair, very lightly. His fingers never touched her skin. She watched the softening of his face, and the gentle motion of his rough hand over the springy texture of her hair was wonderfully soothing. "I mean it, Joey," he said. "For the next couple of days don't worry about anything. Just rest and get your head together."

Her expression was closer to a weak grimace than a smile. "It'll take longer than a couple of days for that, I'm afraid."

"Then," he advised soberly, "take as long as you need."

What a beautiful invitation. What comforting words, and all the more so because Jo Ella knew that he meant it. At that moment nothing looked better to her than simply to sit back and do nothing, to relax and let Cam take care of her—for as long as it took. She had fought hard, she was tired. And instinctively, Cam knew just what to give her. Time, all that she needed, with no place to go and nothing to do. For the first time in her life she welcomed it.

Cam let his hand drop from her hair; he sat back. "Your mother said you'd been working in some kind of insurance office."

Jo Ella nodded. "Clerical work, part-time. It was something to pass the days, and it helped Mom a little with the bills." But then a shadow crossed over her eyes and she repressed a shudder. "God, it was terrible. That dusty little closet they put me in, nothing to do but file day after day.... I thought I'd go mad. And of course after a while word got around—about why I was home, and people started looking at me."

Cam restrained the urge to reach for her, to offer her

a stronger comfort than that of the gentle but impersonal touches he had given her before now. Her spirit had taken a battering, all right, and it hurt him to see her like this. It hurt him to imagine what she had been through.

Then she lowered her eyes, as though she did not want him to see the pain there. "Mom cashed in an insurance policy to pay my legal fees," she said quietly.

Cam was silent for a moment, and when he spoke his tone was impartial and unsurprised. "And you feel guilty about that."

"Not only that," Jo Ella admitted reluctantly, studying her swollen toes.

"But the fact that you hated every minute you had to be there, you hated every sympathetic look and every pep talk and every gesture of support."

Jo Ella looked up at him in surprise. "Yes."

He smiled. "She was smothering you. You always said she did that to you, ever since you were a kid. You've always seen her love as a kind of weapon against you, something to keep you tied down. But it's not really that way, Joey," he reminded her gently. "Mothers can't help being mothers. And love doesn't have to be a cage."

Jo Ella lowered her eyes. He was right, she knew. She resented her mother for the very things she should have loved her for, and it had always been that way. It probably had something to do with being the youngest and the last to leave the nest; it probably had a lot more to do with growing up in a family of nine and having to fight tooth and nail for every bit of personal space and each scrap of privacy. It just seemed as though everything her mother did for her was designed to make Jo Ella feel guilty for not being a more dutiful daughter, and it worked.

She lifted her eyebrows in a baffled, dismissing gesture, saying merely, "Interpersonal relationships are very complicated things."

"Which is precisely," he returned lightly, rising, "why you've always avoided them. Dibs on the shower."

Jo Ella had a retort on the tip of her tongue, but she never said it. She merely watched him leave the room, and then she wondered why Cam had never married.

He was in all other respects the epitome of the average American male. Student body president and valedictorian in high school, two years of college, exemplary service record, a model citizen. He had never been in a fight or been seen falling-down drunk or even gotten a traffic ticket. Even in the reckless teenage years it was Burt who would call from jail and usually Cam who would go bail him out. Cam always left before the parties got too wild. He led a very conservative, upright, perfectly middle-of-the-road life. Cam simply did not believe in breaking the rules. By all that was logical, he should have been married with at least two children by now, a house in the suburbs and two gas-guzzling cars. Nothing would have made him happier.

It was not that he by any means led the life of a monk, and most of his relationships were relatively long-term. The last one had lasted almost three years. Jo Ella knew that she was not the first woman to move in here, and that she would not be the last. And that realization made her sad, somehow, and a little confused.

Cam had been standing there, watching her, for a long time before she sensed his presence. He was wondering what had possessed him to do such a crazy thing as invite her to move in here. At the time it had seemed as though he had waited all his life for an opportunity like this; for the time Jo Ella would need him and he would be able to be there for her, to fill an emptiness, to offer her something she couldn't do without. To have a place in her life for a time. But he was already beginning to see that it was a rash and foolish decision motivated by air-filled daydreams and that he had really gained nothing—except perhaps more heartache. He had made a mistake with her once, and he valued himself too much to risk his emotions again.

Cam had not been Jo Ella's first lover, he knew that. But none of the beauty had been lost from one idyllic spring because of it. Now he wondered unaccountably how many there had been since him. He wondered if she ever thought of him, and if she remembered, as he did.

It was his scent that first alerted Jo Ella, in her half-dozing state, to his presence. Tangy soap and shower steam, a warm and familiar scent that made her imagine, for the briefest of moments, what it would be like to be wrapped in male arms still heated from the water, to be enveloped in the fog of warmth that drifted from his body and from the slippery droplets remaining on his skin. She could almost taste the clean residue of soap on her tongue.

Cam sauntered casually into the room, dressed only

in a beige terry-cloth kimono, with a towel around his neck. His hair was slicked back and still glistening darkly, and he said cheerfully, "Okay, lady, get out of my bed so I can hit the sack. We can celebrate your homecoming another night—I'm really beat."

Jo Ella, sitting up as he scooped up the pillows and blankets, protested, "Now, Cam, I thought we had agreed—"

"Don't be a pain in the neck, Joey." He dumped the blankets on the sofa and pulled the coffee table out of the way. The hairs on his legs were sculpted darkly to lean muscles and sinew that flexed and bunched when he moved. He smelled wonderful. "You're a guest—you're supposed to do what I say."

Jo Ella laughed tiredly and stood up. "I thought it was the other way around—the guest is always right."

"Not in this house." He began to remove the cushions from the sofa. "It'll be much easier to have you safely tucked away in the bedroom—that way I don't have to worry about tripping over your shoes or getting tangled up in your lingerie or getting your perfume mixed up with my after-shave."

Jo Ella couldn't think of an argument for that, so she merely laughed again and bent to help him make up the bed. But as she moved close to him their arms brushed, and he turned quickly to stuff the pillow into a pillowcase. His skin, touching for just that moment against hers, was as warm and steamy as she had imagined. "Don't bother with this," he said, rather abruptly. "It's faster if I do it myself. You go on and get some rest."

Jo Ella looked at him rather uncertainly, but he kept

his back to her. "Okay, then," she agreed after a moment. She turned toward the bedroom. "I'll see you in the morning, Cam."

Still he did not look up. "Night, Joey," was his only reply.

Chapter Five

Jo Ella did not expect to sleep. She hadn't really slept well since this whole thing had begun, and usually she lay awake for hours, trying to calm her perpetually racing mind, waiting for exhaustion to take over. But the trip must have tired her more than she realized, because the last thing she remembered was climbing into Cam's king-sized bed and snuggling her face into a maroon-colored pillowcase that smelled of fabric softener, smiling as she thought of Cam doing a special load of laundry to prepare for her arrival. The labyrinth of antiseptic-smelling hospital corridors did not haunt her that night, the tortured, pleading eyes of Bobby Williams left her in peace. She did not even dream of Cam.

Until she opened her eyes sleepily the next morning and had a fuzzy vision of Cam's face, and beneath it a splash of color shaped like a rose—and she thought she must be dreaming. Then she heard his cheerful voice, in more of a demand than a greeting: "Good morning, sleepyhead!" And she opened her eyes wider.

It really was Cam, with morning sunshine bouncing

off his floppy hair and crinkling his eyes; he was freshly shaved and dressed in jeans and a yellow T-shirt with a drunken armadillo on the front. He was holding a breakfast tray with a rose in a bud vase on it.

Jo Ella struggled to a sitting position, pushing her hair out of her eyes. "Cam! What are you doing?"

"Pampering you." He placed the tray on her lap with a flourish. "This is a four-star hotel, didn't you know that? Breakfast in bed comes with the package—first day only."

"Oh..." She took in the feast before her with steadily widening eyes. Pancakes and honey, link sausages, scrambled eggs, orange juice, coffee—and the rose. She touched it wonderingly. "Where did you get it?"

"It's silk." He grinned, sitting on the edge of the bed beside her. She touched it again and discovered that it was, indeed, silk. "It was on a birthday present that somebody gave me as a joke. The food, however, is real."

"It looks delicious." She took up her fork, her usually sluggish appetite stimulated by the unexpected luxury. "But..." She glanced at him suspiciously. "Last night there was nothing in your refrigerator."

"Most of it came from the freezer," he admitted. "That's how bachelors eat, you know—from the freezer to indigestion in less than fifteen minutes."

She laughed and took a bite of the pancakes. They did not taste indigestible to her at all.

Cam had forgotten how huggable Jo Ella looked in the mornings. Her hair tousled, her skin flushed, her eyes like mirrors. Little pink lines on her shoulder where the crumpled sheet had pressed an indentation, the scoop-necked nightgown with its flowery print and its bit of lace edging just hiding her cleavage. If he looked, he was sure he would be able to see the outline of her nipples beneath the thin cotton. But he wasn't going to look. A sweet, powdery scent floated up from her that reminded him of springtime. This was Jo Ella as he liked her best, and he had forgotten what a delicate and wonderful invasion of the senses she could be first thing in the morning. But there was no point in remembering.

Picking up one of her sausages, he said, "So what are you going to do today?"

Jo Ella took a sip of her juice and sat back against the pillows luxuriously. "Nothing," she replied, and it sounded wonderful to her. "Absolutely nothing."

He winked at her and touched her nose lightly with his forefinger. "Good for you." And then he questioned, "It won't bother you, being here alone?"

Jo Ella gve him a look filled with forbearance, and Cam's grin was a little apologetic. He knew that Jo Ella, of all people, never minded being alone. "Right," he said, and standing up, finished off the sausage. "I'll see you about six, then. I'll give you a call sometime during the day, okay?"

And then, because it seemed like the natural thing to do, he bent and brushed her cheek with a kiss. The closeness of him, the feel of his warmth enveloping her and the smoothness of his face against her cheek for just that brief moment sent Jo Ella back in time. The boundaries of years and distance wavered and blurred, and her instinct was to place her hands on his arms and to turn her mouth to his.... But of course she didn't. She simply smiled, although it might have been a little uncertainly, and she said, "Sure. Okay. I'll be here."

He looked at her for another moment, and behind the smile in his eyes she thought she saw something else. A softening or a deepening, or perhaps even a flash of pain. But it was gone in an instant, and he straightened up. "See you later, Joey," he called as he left the room.

When she heard the front door close behind him, Jo Ella lifted her fingers to her cheek where his lips had touched so quickly, so impersonally, and she let them linger there for a moment. Then she smiled at her own silliness and turned back to her breakfast with only slightly less enthusiasm.

IT WAS A LONG, LAZY DAY, and Jo Ella reveled in it. She did the breakfast dishes and her morning exercises, made her bed and settled down to watch a talk show. She unpacked and hung her clothes on the opposite side of the double closet from Cam's. Cam had left her a set of keys, so she felt free to change into jogging shorts and run through the apartment complex for forty-five minutes; then she came back and took a nap. In the afternoon there was an old movie on local TV, and she enjoyed it thoroughly. She could not remember when she had ever been so self-indulgent or aimless, and it was a new and welcome experience to her. She had nothing to do. No place to go. No demands were being made on her at all except that she sit back and relax. She didn't even think. There were things that needed to be analyzed, she knew, decisions to be made and values to be rearranged, but today she escaped them all. And she loved every minute of it.

She took a long bubble bath, shampooed her hair, and changed into a comfortable, floor-length sundress in an airy flowered print. She even applied a little perfume and manicured her nails, just for the fun of pampering herself. At five-thirty she decided the least she could do to repay Cam for the breakfast surprise was to warm up the leftovers his mother had so thoughtfully prepared, and she set about doing it.

When Cam came in a little after six o'clock, the table was set with a linen tablecloth and napkins that obviously hadn't been used since the last time his mother came to visit, stoneware plates with a blue ships-at-sea etching, and two slender blue candles that Jo Ella had found on the top shelf of the utility closet. The apartment was fragrant with the lilac scent of the candles and his mother's cooking, and Cameron stopped midway into the room, his eyes widening in wonder. "What in the world..." he exclaimed softly. His eyes lifted to hers in amazement. "Did you *cook*?"

Jo Ella laughed with a delighted pleasure at his reaction. "Not exactly," she assured him, setting a platter on the table. "I just warmed up last night's meal."

"Hey, you didn't have to do that." He tossed his jacket on the armchair and came slowly into the dining area, but the expression in his eyes made Jo Ella very glad she had. "We could have gone out for something."

"And let all this food go to waste? Come on, everything's ready. Sit down."

But first he held Jo Ella's chair for her, and the clean,

fresh scent of him wafted over her. She felt just exactly like a woman who had invited a man she wanted to impress home for dinner, and she had never done anything like that in her life. It was a nice feeling, warm and feminine and rather exciting, like a first date.

"You even found the wine," he marveled, and went around the table to pour it. He paused and lifted his glass to her before he sat down, and his eyes were warm and sparkling and bottomless. "To a gorgeous little lady," he said, "and one hell of a cook."

Jo Ella laughed and returned the toast. "To your mother."

Cam entertained her with stories about the oil tycoon, a regular customer of theirs, who had misplaced his well and kept Burt busy all day flying in a five-mile circle looking for it. Jo Ella watched the candlelight play on his face and the soft sweep of his hair, and every once in a while, during a pause in the conversation, she caught a look in his eyes that was so warm, so endearing and so filled with pleasure that it took her breath away.

"This is great, Joey," he said at last, pushing his plate away. The expression on his face told her he really meant it; he was relaxed, content and still a little awed. "Do you know how long it's been since I had a real meal at my own table?"

Jo Ella laughed and sipped her wine. "It doesn't take much to make you happy, does it?"

"I'm a man of simple tastes," he agreed, eyes twinkling. "A hot meal after a long day at work, a good-looking woman across the table, a fine cigar . . ." With a mischievous glance at her, he pulled a long cigar out of his pocket.

"Oh, Cam," she protested, her nose wrinkling in distaste, "you're not going to light that thing!"

"Watch me." He leaned forward to bring the tip of his cigar to the candle flame, but Jo Ella did not stay to watch. She took the dishes to the kitchen.

When the dishwasher was humming softly, the countertops sparkling and the automatic coffeemaker set to prepare Cam's coffee before he got up the next morning, Jo Ella turned off the lights and left the kitchen, pleased with a good day's job of doing nothing. Cam had extinguished the candles and turned on a single yellow lamp in the living room; he beckoned her from the sofa.

It was a beautiful, quiet cozy scene. Soft light, the sound of the dishwasher in the background, and Cam waiting for her. It made Jo Ella suddenly think about all the things her life had been missing, even before it had undergone this drastic upheaval. She had never realized before what a lonely life she led. It was filled with people, true, people who cared about her and depended on her, and people she cared about in return. It had been, at least to this point, busy and demanding and satisfying, and if she had ever started to get bored, it had been easy enough to move on. But there was never anyone to come home to.

The cigar lay extinguished in the ashtray, and Jo Ella lifted an eyebrow as she came over to him. "What happened to the fine cigar?"

"It seems to taste better mixed with machine oil and engine exhaust," he confessed. "The smell is a bit much for a small apartment."

She sat beside him, and his arm very naturally encircled her shoulders, making it easy for her to rest her head against him. It felt good. Snug and cozy and comfortable. As though they had been doing it all their lives. "Don't you ever get the urge," she inquired thoughtfully, "to fly those helicopters, instead of just taking them apart?"

"I also put them back together," he pointed out. Then he shook his head. "No. I'm a builder, not a flier. Somebody has to keep his feet on the ground, you know."

A small, reflective smile touched Jo Ella's lips. That was Cam, all right. Always the ground crew, keeping things in order, always ready with sound advice or navigational information while she went flying around on her perpetual missions. Always there when she got back, waiting to repair the damage and set her up for the next flight. There were the doers and the watchers; Cam was a watcher. Jo Ella had never before clearly understood the interdependence between the two, what an important part those quiet, stable, gently plodding people were to the overall function of life. They gave people like Jo Ella the freedom to dream while they went determinedly and unobtrusively about the job of maintaining the status quo.

"But," she said, shaking her head softly, "I'd go crazy."

"I know you would," he agreed quietly. That sounded like a note of sadness in his voice, and Jo Ella did not want to lift her face to make sure.

But the mood had subtly shifted, both of them thinking about things of a more serious nature than they would have liked. Cam's fingers traced a light, absent pattern on the bare flesh of Jo Ella's upper arm, and his calloused fingertips made her skin tingle. She tried not to think how it had once been between them. She tried not to wonder if it would be different now.

But something made her say, forcing lightness into her tone, "How long has it been, anyway, since some woman fixed dinner for you at your own table?"

The absent stroking motions of his fingers stopped; his hand moved very slowly to the back of her neck. A slight pressure made her turn her face to look at him.

His expression was sober, his eyes a very deep green. Jo Ella's throat felt dry and she could feel the faint veil of a flush spread over her body, pushed forward by the steadily increasing rhythm of her pulse. The moment in which he looked at her seemed suspended in uncertainty and anticipation, a promise barely withheld, a need that couldn't be disguised. Her lips were parted, but she forgot to breathe. Her eyes met his, and she couldn't blink. She felt certain he was going to kiss her. And she wanted him to, very badly.

He said softly, "A long time." His eyes dropped slowly toward her lips. Jo Ella wanted to do something, to say something, to touch him or to move toward him; to let him know that she would welcome him. But something prevented her. Perhaps it was because she knew instinctively, better than anyone else, that in matters of the heart freedom of choice cannot be impaired.

Then he smiled and moved away, reaching for the remote control. "Let's see what's on television," he suggested.

Jo Ella swallowed back disappointment with a smile.

But the smile was rather weak, and the emotion that caused the sinking feeling in the pit of her stomach was sharper than disappointment. She felt as though she had reached for a lifeline in the midst of a turbulent sea and her grasping fingers had missed it by inches. Cam did not want her anymore.

And she knew why.

It was probably for the best, she knew. She could not afford to get involved with anyone right now when her life was in such turmoil, especially not Cam. This living arrangement had been offered out of friendship, and a sexual relationship would complicate it beyond all reason. Why was she setting herself up for more emotional stress? She should have known better than to think she could sail back into Cam's life and pick up something that had been dropped seven years ago. He could be in love with someone else by now. She hadn't even bothered to find out about that, to ask if her presence here was cramping his style—and that was typically selfish of her.

No wonder Cam didn't want her. She had swept into his life without giving a single thought to the inconvenience or distress it might cause him. What was it doing to Cam, so moral and upright, to be harboring in his house a woman whom most people believed to be the lowest kind of criminal? No wonder he could hardly bear to look at her. What kind of battle had he undergone with his conscience before calling her, what had it cost him to let loyalty to an old friend win over his better judgment? What was it costing him now?

They sat side by side on the sofa, no longer even touching. Cam had gradually moved away, pretending absorption with the television program, so that not even their arms were brushing. Jo Ella felt the chill of the wall that was rising between them. She said, "I think I'll check out some employment agencies tomorrow."

He glanced at her, then pushed the button on the remote control that lowered the television volume. As always, he was ready to give her his attention when she needed it. "Anything particular in mind?" he inquired.

No, she answered him silently. *Just to stop imposing on you....* She shook her head. "I don't think it will be in medicine, though."

He nodded, as though that came as no great surprise to him. And his gaze was very thoughtful. "Look, Joey," he said after a moment, "I know how you feel about sitting around doing nothing, and you were probably bored as hell around here all day—"

"No," she interrupted quickly, and the swift truth of it surprised her. "No, as a matter of fact, I enjoyed it." She laughed a little self-consciously. "For the first time in my life, I guess, I really had fun just doing nothing. Maybe I'm getting old." And she glanced at him, a little shyly, hoping he would read the unspoken message there. "Or growing up," she added softly.

He looked at her as though he could not be quite sure whether or not to believe her, as though trying to decide whether the sentiment was genuine or merely motivated out of politeness. "The thing is," he said carefully, "you've been through a rough time. Maybe this is not the best time for you to be rushing into career decisions, and I don't want you to feel pressured. When I made the offer, I meant for you to stay with me as long as you wanted—even after you're working, if you like."

Jo Ella was confused. He seemed very genuine, but that was just Cam's way. He would never do anything to hurt anyone's feelings or make anyone feel unwelcome. She wanted very badly to take what he said at face value, to believe he meant it and to relax with it. But she said patiently, "Cam, let's be honest. You were sweet to offer and I'll always appreciate it, but it *is* an imposition on you. You can't go on sleeping on the sofa indefinitely, and feeding me and sheltering me out of the goodness of your heart. And what about your social life?" Now she had said it, the thing she really wanted to know. But she kept her expression carefully neutral. "What if you want to bring some woman home one night—what is she going to say about your roommate? Of course it's inconvenient for you."

"There is no woman," he told her plainly, "that I want to bring home." His eyes were clear, his expression open and unaffected. "Does that make you feel more comfortable?"

Not really. Because there was something in Cam's eyes, or perhaps in his tone of voice, that suggested to Jo Ella that he knew her interest in that part of his life was motivated by more than just a friendly desire to be helpful. And it embarrassed her. She lowered her eyes briefly. "Still..."

"I'd personally like to see you just keep on doing nothing for a while," he told her, and his expression was very frank, "until you've decided what you really want. And don't think you're a burden on me—financial or otherwise, because it's simply not true."

Now she managed a nervous little laugh. "Come on, Cam, I can't let you just go on 'keeping' me while I sit around and do nothing! It could get to be a habit."

"Then let it," he suggested easily. He made it sound so simple. "Don't you think," he added, his expression gentling, "that there's enough history between us to allow that?"

Jo Ella met his eyes, and she knew then that he had not forgotten. It was all there, the tenderness, the sorrow, the gentle remembrance of what might have been, and it pulled at Jo Ella's heart. She wanted nothing more at that moment than to give her soul to the care that sprang from the depths of those gentle eyes, to let herself be enfolded in the embrace of his strong arms, to take certainty and security from the steady beating of his heart. Oh, yes. There was history there. But no future.

All she said, shifting her eyes away from him, was "We'll see how it goes."

Jo Ella made herself stay up with him and pretend to watch the rest of the movie, but she could not have told anyone later what it was about. Cam was relaxed and comfortable, for he rarely wasted energy worrying about things he could not change. But Jo Ella felt a heavy depression seeping over her, made all the more difficult because she could not share it with Cam. She didn't think this was going to work, as much as she would like to pretend otherwise.

They said good night casually, as they had before, nothing more than friends. Jo Ella fell into a restless sleep to the background murmur of the late evening news coming from the other room.

For a time Jo Ella didn't think she was sleeping at all. The voices coming from the other room grew more muted and then seem to change, to become intermingled with other voices, among them her own, cheerful and professional: "Well, Mr. Williams, what brings you to our fine establishment?"

And a young man's voice, equally optimistic: "Just a little stomach virus...I'll have this thing beat in no time."

Jo Ella's voice again, floating with a teasing lilt through the dim, echoing clamor of other voices: "That's too bad; we like to keep the cute ones around awhile...."

And more clearly now, the anxious voice of a young wife: "Bobby will be all right, won't he?"

Then his parents, louder now: "He'll be all right, won't he?" and louder still, "*He'll be all right, won't he*?" then tumbling over one another, louder and louder, echoing and pounding at her like the relentless surge of the tide that attacks the shore, "He'll be all right, won't he? He'll be all right? *He'll be*..."

And then Jo Ella knew she was dreaming because she could see the fuzzy beige walls of the hospital room, she could see dull and tortured eyes, she could feel the clasp of a cold dry hand on hers. That hand that had once been so strong and tanned, now wasted to tissue-paper flesh over a skeleton that was as fragile as twigs, now gripping her fingers with the strength of a two-day-old infant. She could hear the bleep of the monitor in the background, the hum of the oxygen. And she heard her own voice, gentle, reassuring, "You're going to be all right, Bobby. You're going to be all right."

And she knew she was dreaming because the walls of the room slowly began to blur and move, the sharp mechanical beeps of the monitor grew louder and louder, measuring every beat of her heart as the walls moved closer...and the grip on her hand tightened, tightened, hurting her fingers. She tried to pull away but she couldn't, he held her hand and she couldn't get away, she couldn't breathe, the walls were so close. He was crushing her fingers, he wouldn't let her go, she couldn't get away, no matter how hard she pulled he held her firm. The walls were crushing her. The monitor was screaming at her. She couldn't breathe. "Let me go," she gasped, trying to twist away. "Let me..."

"Let me go," Jo Ella whispered aloud. "Let me go...."

Jo Ella opened her eyes to the gradually swimming arrangement of unfamiliar walls and unfamiliar furnishings, a twilight dark, but not the hospital room. Thank God, not the hospital room. She pushed herself up slowly with arms that felt like rubber, taking a deep breath of clean, unscented air. There was a thin line of perspiration on her upper lip and she was cold.

She got out of bed a little unsteadily, pulling on her wrapper and hugging it close. She tiptoed to the bathroom, trying not to wake Cam.

She splashed cold water on her face, trying to wash away the residue of the dream. She basked in the bright fluorescence of the bathroom light and the worst of the nightmare faded away. But she knew she would not sleep again tonight.

Jo Ella passed silently through the living room, where the sound of Cam's deep, regular breathing assured her she had not disturbed him. And she had to pause a few feet away from the sofa bed, just to look at him, taking comfort in the quiet security of his presence.

The filtering streetlight screened the room with a gray-blue opalescence that bathed Cam's sleeping figure. He slept sprawled out like a child, half on his side and half on his stomach, one arm stretched over the width of the bed, the other cushioning his cheek. The blanket outlined his long figure from the waist down but his torso was bare. Jo Ella knew he slept in the nude. His bare shoulders, amber-tan in other light, appeared almost pearly, and Jo Ella could see the pattern of freckles on his left shoulder that was shaped like a flock of birds in flight. How many times had she traced that V-pattern with her fingertips, teasing him, laughing with him, arousing him.... His hair fell soft and bouncy around his face, its muted glow caught in places by the surrealistic light and reflecting silver. She could see the gentle rise and fall of his chest and his back with each breath. There was warmth, and security, and strong arms to hold her and keep the nightmares at bay.... She turned away.

Jo Ella slid open the balcony door with a muffled creak and stepped outside. The air was cool, and though a moment ago she had been cold, it now felt good against her warm cheeks. She took a deep breath, drawing the cleansing nighttime into her lungs. The stars overhead were like bits of phosphorus, and the Texas sky went on forever. A person could lose himself in the brilliance and vastness of a Texas sky.

She had never thought she would return here. She

had never made any concrete plans against it, it was simply that she had never imagined that the most important crisis of her life would be played out in the state of her birth, with all her past mistakes to witness it. It was like coming full circle, as though Fate in its infinite wisdom had conspired to bring her back home just when she had forgotten where home was.

In the past five years she had lived in twenty-seven states and two foreign countries, not counting the ports of call made on the cruise ship. She always kept an eye out for short-term private-duty assignments, and she had contacts who made sure she was first on the list for those companies with branches overseas that imported their own medical teams for their personnel. The Austin job had just been a stopgap until something better came along. It was a hospital in which she had worked before, and she knew they would hire her, the pay was good and she had nothing against Texas. But she was just marking time until she could move on. And suddenly time stood still.

She did not know why it had to happen in this time, in this place, with this patient. She had been witness to other tragedies, she had played out her crucial role in other dramas just as poignant, just as gripping, as Bobby's. She had jotted down the time of death on charts of newborns, young wives in the prime of life, sage old men whose passing would leave a gap in the lives of all those around them, and each time it had hurt her, each time she had felt a tug of loss against her spirit from theirs. She had done two months' duty in a large urban emergency room, and she had seen every kind of atrocity that could be inflicted on the human body, and she had never grown immune. She had given a part of herself to every one of her patients, and there had been thousands. She did not know why it had had to culminate with Bobby Williams, in this time, in this place.

Or perhaps that was just it. It was a culmination of all the helplessness and all the suffering, all the standing by silently and watching lives slip away. Maybe it was a lesson of some sort.

She heard the balcony door squeak open, and Cam stood beside her. She glanced at him, forcing an uncertain little half smile. "Sorry," she said softly. "I didn't mean to wake you."

He said nothing, just stood beside her, strong and steady and secure. Just being there.

He was wearing only the short beige robe, and the triangle of his bare chest was a lighter shadow in the starlight. His hands were pushed into the front pockets of the robe, drawing the material taut over his buttocks. He looked out over the sleeping buildings and the quiet drives below them, and he looked rested and peaceful. There was nothing about him to indicate that he had been awakened in the middle of the night from a sound sleep; not even his hair was tousled. It fell as smooth and straight as cashmere, shaping his head, brushing his neck, just shadowing his left eye. He looked beautiful to Jo Ella, simply because he was there.

"It smells good out here," he said in a moment, quietly. "Sweet." And then he glanced at her, smiling. "Or is that you?"

An alien shyness crept over Jo Ella, a fluttering sensation whose main source seemed to be the very molecules of her skin. Her eyes shifted away from his with a little shrug of her shoulders; she stepped over to the rail.

Jo Ella looked out over the parking lot, at the darkened windowpanes of sleeping apartments, the stillness of palm trees standing like sentinels along the drives. Cam leaned his hip against the rail and looked in the opposite direction, toward his empty apartment. The silence they shared was kind and undemanding, like the night itself.

Cam said quietly, after a time, "I just want you to know I'm here, if you ever want to talk about it."

Jo Ella caught her breath against a sudden misty sting of tears, and then blinked them back determinedly. Yes, Cam would always be there. He would listen. And she wanted to talk to him, she wanted him to understand. She took a breath, flattening her palms against the rail, stiffening her arms; then she tried to smile. "We used to bet on football games, you know?" Her voice was a little tight. "Bobby and I. Sometimes when I was off duty I would come over and watch the games with him.... He always won, of course, because he knew the players and the teams so much better than I did. He liked Def Leppard and Chinese art. Can you believe that?" A little laugh stammered in her throat. "A guy like that, into Chinese art..." But then the laugh got caught somewhere in her chest, threatening to choke her, and the sound that emerged felt more like a sob. She felt Cam's hand, warm and comforting, fall upon her shoulder.

She stiffened herself against the pain, dropping her

head. The landscape below her blurred hotly once, then cleared again with a blink of her eyes. "Damn it," she said fiercely, "it shouldn't have happened. A healthy young man—his whole life before him—he had *colitis*, for God's sake. Nobody dies from colitis. He should have been in and out of there in a week, he should have..."

Cam drew her slowly into his arms, holding her lightly against his chest, his hands stroking her back soothingly, comfortingly. Jo Ella's voice was broken and muffled against the soft fabric of his robe. "Should have had kids and gone to the Super-Bowl, should have had a big house with lots of trees and played football with his son on the front lawn. He should have—" But she couldn't talk anymore, because if she did that awful dam of tears in her chest would break through and she would be out of control; she couldn't talk anymore because she didn't want Cam to hear the rest, she couldn't do that to him.

So she just let Cam hold her and she took long, unsteady breaths that gradually pushed the nightmare away. She let his warmth soothe her and his strength support her; she felt the beat of his heart against her cheek and the smoothness of his flesh against her face, and that was her comfort.

The night grew calm around them, and the storm that was threatening to break within Jo Ella found quiescence. Her breathing grew steady and the aching in her chest slowly abated. It felt so good, just standing there in the circle of Cam's arms. Her hands curled around the lapels of his robe, her heated face drew a neutral temperature from the cool night air. The muscles of his chest felt hard against her face, but the skin that covered them was soft and smooth. The scent of his hair drifted over her with an ephemeral air current, clean and fresh, like stored sunshine. His strong fingers were quiet on her back, just holding her, protecting her, and the passage of his breath was soothing and even. It mesmerized the rhythm of her heart.

Jo Ella said softly, without lifting her face to look at him, "Do you remember that time I tried to jump off the roof of the toolshed?"

The small sound Cam made deep in his throat was of wry reminiscence. "Remember? I've still got the scar. You were going to jump from the roof to the branch of the oak tree a few yards away, only the branch broke—"

"And you caught me," Jo Ella said, still not looking at him.

Again Cam's grunt was of low amusement. "Sure did. Two broken ribs and a dislocated shoulder, and all you got was the wind knocked out of you. Not one of the brightest moves I ever made in my life."

Jo Ella tried to laugh; it came out a little choked. Her hands tightened imperceptibly on his lapels. "Me either, come to think of it."

"It would have been quite a stunt if it had worked, though," Cam argued mildly. And then his voice grew more thoughtful. "You made such a picture.... Sometimes I can still see you, poised on top of that roof, the sun in your hair and the sky as big as the universe around you, ready to take off into space with no doubt in the world that you could fly."

And then Jo Ella tilted her face to look at him, smiling. "Is that," she asked softly, "why you always call me your little bird?"

Cam shook his head. His eyes were soft and opaque, and he seemed to be very far away. "No," he answered slowly. "That's from something I read somewhere... about not being able to say a bird belongs to you until you let it go, and it flies back to you of its own free will." Then he smiled at her, his eyes clearing, and he shrugged a little. "Silly, I guess."

Jo Ella met his gaze, a strange and wonderful contentment stealing through her. She lifted her hand and lightly touched the small scar just above his temple, close to the hairline, where the falling branch had struck him so many years ago. And she whispered, "No. Not silly at all."

She felt the slight stiffening of his muscles when she touched him, which could have been no more than the brief cessation of his breath. She saw, far back in his eyes, a glow of gentle wonder begin to kindle; his fingers tightened on her back ever so slightly, swaying her toward him. His lashes dropped as in slow motion to hood the glow in his eyes, and by inches, as though fighting a compulsion he could not disobey, his face moved toward hers.

His lips fell upon hers, a gentle warmth of sparkling electricity that danced like stars behind Jo Ella's closed eyes. She felt that warmth fan slowly through her, stealing across her face and flooding her throat, jarring her pulse and weakening her knees. No one had ever been able to do that to her but Cam. No one had ever kissed her like Cam. It hadn't changed, they hadn't lost it....

His hands moved across her back, thumbs sliding into her armpits and strong fingers splayed across her shoulder blades, drawing her closer as his kiss deepened. She could feel the thud of his heart against her breast, and it seemed to be only an echo of the slamming rhythm of her own heartbeat as her lips parted beneath his and his tongue slipped inside. Dewy moistness, electric jolts, breath-robbing, mind-twisting pleasure, he seemed to invade all of her, to swallow her up in his own overwhelming vibrance. His muscles hardened as hers turned to water, he drew her energy into his strength, he made her a part of him. And she flowed into him as naturally as a stream seeking its source, thoughtlessly, helplessly, joyously.

She felt the pressure of Cam's thumbs against the curve of her breasts, the hardness of his chest, the heat that swept from him and mingled with her own. Trembling fingers explored the curve of his ear, the tingling texture of his hair, the strong breadth of his neck. She tasted him, she blended into him, she was filled with him. The soft moan that came deep from his throat could have been a sound of surrender as, briefly, he pressed her to him, fingers curving tightly around her shoulders, tongue searching and drawing and deepening—and then, gently but deliberately withdrawing.

Cam's lips lingered on hers, his tongue swept their curves. The grip of his fingers began to loosen; his breath brushed across her mouth, cooling the moisture there. His hands drifted down her back and rested at last, very lightly, on her waist. He stepped back.

Jo Ella could not let him go. Her muscles were rubbery, her skin still tingling, her heart thundering erratic pulses of weakness and confusion through her brain. The breath that whispered through her lungs was sluggish and shallow, and her entire being was drawn toward his touch, for separateness from him was alien to her. Her fingers curled around his collar, her eyes questioned and urged; she whispered, "Cam..."

"No." His voice was a little hoarse, though he meant it to be gentle. She could see, in the dimness, the taut muscles of his neck, the prominent ridges that outlined the hollow of his throat. There was a faint sheen of perspiration on his face, the residual flush of heat—and his eyes were perfectly blank. He dropped his hands from her waist. "I think..." he said, and his voice was not quite even. His eyes shifted away from her. "I think you'd better go back to bed... and try to get some rest."

Very slowly, Jo Ella's arms fell from around his neck. She felt weak, exhausted, drained, and a little numb, as though she had just run a marathon in record time. She rested her hand on the rail behind her for support, trying to subdue the pain that his words had stabbed in to her stomach and was blossoming slowly in her chest. Hurt and confusion chased each other around in her mind, and every time her heart beat against her chest it felt like a new outbreak of tears. He didn't want her.

Cam strained to bring his breathing under control. He watched the pain and the sense of betrayal rise up in Jo Ella's eyes and had to clench his fists at his sides to keep from reaching for her. She would not know how much it cost him to step away from her. He knew she needed him tonight, but not as much as he needed her.

She needed the comfort his body could bring her, for tonight or a series of nights or however long it took for her to recover herself, and he needed... what?

Whatever it was, it was more than she could give him. And more than he could ask of her.

Jo Ella half turned from him, and her hand tightened on the rail. Her voice was low and not quite even, and she said simply, "It's because of Bobby, isn't it? Because of what happened and what they said—"

"No!" His voice was harsh. The tension exploded in a rush as his hand closed around her arm, making her look at him. His eyes were very dark, the lines of his face hard. "No, don't ever think that. Nothing anyone could say would ever—" And with a breath, he forced gentleness into his tone. "That has nothing to do with us, Joey," he said, and he slowly released her arm. His face softened, and so did his voice. "It's just that—right now you're in no condition to know what you want or don't want, and I can't let us use each other like that. Do you understand?"

Jo Ella did not understand. She was not certain she believed him, though she wanted to. She wanted to believe that nothing had changed between them, that he did not despise her or harbor secret suspicions about her—that he only thought the best of her and wanted the best for her, just as he always had done. But she wasn't sure.

She made herself smile, she forced strength into her trembling limbs. Whatever Cam wanted, that was all that mattered. She had to accept it.

She drew her robe more tightly around her and

turned to go inside. Cam said quietly, "Good night, Joey."

At the door, she turned to look at him. Standing strong and silent in the night, an oak that never bent with the wind. The emotion that twisted in her stomach was half pain and half wonder; it took her back almost twenty years and it surprised her, because it hadn't changed at all since then. "You always caught me," she said softly.

He met her eyes for a moment, and she thought she saw a flicker of something from the past—a tenderness or a yearning, a moment come and gone too quickly to be recaptured. Then she slid the door open and stepped inside, leaving him standing there in the dark.

Chapter Six

"But I don't understand, Miss Cable." The woman across the desk from Jo Ella gave her a pleasant, perplexed little smile and adjusted her fashion-tinted glasses on her nose. "You're a highly qualified R.N., but you don't want a position in nursing. Why not?"

Jo Ella restrained the urge to shift restlessly in her seat like a child who had been caught without her homework. Somehow it had seemed to Jo Ella that the whole world knew who she was and why she could no longer work in nursing. It came as something of a shock for her to realize that it was, in fact, only a small-time case with few sensational elements and had rated little beyond hometown publicity. No one knew, or even cared very much, outside her own professional circle. Which was another very excellent reason, Jo Ella decided, to move outside that circle and start putting the whole thing behind her.

And she did not want to relive the story before this efficient-looking woman, in this little orange-and-yellow-canvased cubicle, to the background of clicking typewriters and ringing telephones. Jo Ella merely shrugged, smiled casually and replied, "Professional burnout, I suppose. Long hours, demanding work, few advancement opportunities—a lot of reasons. I just feel it's time for a change."

"Hmm." Mrs. Bernell pushed at her glasses again and glanced over Jo Ella's résumé. "Pity. Well." She looked up. "What do you expect us to be able to find for you? Do you have anything in particular in mind?"

"Whatever you think I'm qualified for." This was a bad way to conduct an interview, Jo Ella knew, even wih an employment agency. Apathy was not a highly sought-after quality on the job market. But Jo Ella had lost interest in the project almost the moment she had walked in the door. She had come because she felt she had to, but her heart was not really in it.

"You're willing to travel, I see," Mrs. Bernell murmured, turning a page of her file. "That's an asset." She looked up with a reassuring smile. "It may take some time, but we'll do our best to place you. The problem is, of course, that you're overqualified for clerical work but you have no executive experience. But don't let that discourage you. We're proud of the fact that our agency handles the most unusual employment opportunities in the city, and I'm sure we'll come up with something."

Take your time, Jo Ella wanted to say, but instead she stood up and offered her hand. "Thank you. I'll be looking forward to hearing from you."

And Jo Ella couldn't wait to get outside the building, where she breathed deeply of the fresh morning air and hoped she never had to go into another office like that again.

She didn't know what she was going to do. If being in an office for the length of a single interview oppressed her, how did she think she would ever be able to work in one from nine to five or longer? She remembered that awful experience in the cramped back office of the insurance agency. And that was only four hours a day, three days a week. She would go crazy. But what other job opportunities were available to her? And what did she really want?

If I knew that, Jo Ella thought, trying to push away despondency, *I wouldn't be here.*

Or maybe, she realized as she turned the car automatically in the direction of Cam's apartment, she was here because this *was* what she wanted. She was perfectly free, on this sunny, bright October morning, to go sight-seeing or window-shopping or just driving aimlessly around the city. Or for that matter, she could simply drive on through the city limits and beyond, out to whatever adventure awaited her. But without thinking about it at all, without even troubling herself to make a conscious decision, she instinctively turned home. Home. Maybe that was all she wanted, all she needed right now. Just a place to rest and feel welcome.

Welcome. That was the key word. Her mind went back to last night—not only the conversation, but the events afterward. Cam had gone out of his way to tell her she was welcome, and Jo Ella had no doubt that he meant it, or that at least he wanted to mean it. She was welcome in his home as a friend, to take shelter and food and companionship from him until she was strong enough to stand on her own, and that should be enough for her. It was more than she had any right to ask. But last night in his arms she had discovered the beginning of something else, and she had enough foresight to see that they had opened the door on a complication neither of them could afford.

And it wasn't as though she hadn't known it all along, as though it had not been there all the time, just waiting to be discovered—waiting for them to stir the embers of something that should have burned out long ago. Who had done it? Who had rekindled sparks that should have been better left alone, who had made the first move to bring to life a passion that should have been allowed to die a natural and unremarkable death of slow neglect? It must have been Jo Ella. It must have been she who couldn't leave well enough alone, who just couldn't let go and let nature take its course—Jo Ella, who simply could not stop playing God.

It was a mistake, of course. Cam did not want her, that was clear enough. He didn't want the complications she would bring into his life, and she couldn't blame him for that. And she would not force herself where she was not wanted, she would not crowd in on someone else's space.

But she did not know what she was going to do.

For today, all she could do was go on as though nothing had changed. She could go on being a good guest and an easy companion, making no demands on him and being grateful for what he had so generously offered. She would forget the passion that had stirred so briefly and so fiercely between them last night, and she would stop thinking about the time it had lasted longer. She could stop wanting things she couldn't have, and she could try to make this as easy on both of them as possible. For the time being, she had no other choice.

Jo Ella was restless when she arrived back home a little before noon. The apartment seemed very empty without Cam. She changed into her jogging shorts and ran for a while, but that only used up a fraction of her energy. She knew she had to find something to keep her busy or she would start thinking again, and there were too many things lurking in the back of her mind that she simply could not afford to think about.

Because Cam had seemed so pleased when she had dinner ready for him when he came home last night, Jo Ella decided to try it again. Despite her mother's best efforts, Jo Ella had never really learned to cook—there were always too many more exciting things to do, and she was always so fidgety in the kitchen that her mother had finally declared her a hopeless case and barred her from cooking lessons entirely. Not that Jo Ella had ever felt the loss. She knew how to read instructions on a package and set the oven timer, and that was all a person really needed in the modern world of meal preparation. Kitchens had always seemed too confining to Jo Ella, and the less time spent there the better.

But she had reached a point in her life where the absence of domestic accomplishments seemed like a handicap, and she now had plenty of time to broaden her education. She called Cam's mother.

"Well, hello, dear," Avis's pleasant voice greeted her after Jo Ella identified herself. "How are you today?"

"I'm just fine, Mrs. Scott." Jo Ella settled back with

her legs swung over the arm of the easy chair, a note pad braced against her knees, ready to jot down Cam's favorite recipe. "And yourself?"

"Oh, I'm just worried to death about Janice and Matthew," Avis replied in a weary tone, and Jo Ella frowned a little. Did she know them? "He's been offered that high-paying job in Chicago, you know, and I just don't see how he can turn it down."

"Oh," Jo Ella said. "Well," she offered helpfully, "maybe he shouldn't. With the job market the way it is, he could be missing a real opportunity if he's not willing to transfer."

"I suppose," agreed Avis reluctantly. "But there's something awfully suspicious about that Bartlett character."

"Who's Bartlett?" inquired Jo Ella politely. She was still trying to figure out who Janice and Matthew were.

"The man he'll be working for. He's got shifty eyes. Besides, if Janice goes back to Chicago, there'll be trouble, you mark my word."

It was typical of Avis to involve herself so completely in her neighbors' affairs. Jo Ella could not really consider it gossip, since she did not know any of the people involved and couldn't care less what happened to them, so she asked, rather absently, "What kind of trouble?" She didn't know what else to say, since Avis obviously wanted to talk about it. All Jo Ella really wanted was a recipe.

"Well, my dear," Avis confided, "you know Janice was in love with Hilda and Richard's boy—what was his name? Adam, yes, that was it—long before she ever met Matthew. He was a charmer, too, and very good-looking. Well, he went away to Chicago about the time Matthew came to town, and they have such a happy marriage now I'd just hate to see anything break it up."

"Chicago is a big town, Mrs. Scott," Jo Ella assured her. "I'm sure they'll never even run into each other. Now, what I called about—"

"I hope you're right," Avis murmured. "But I still think he'd be making a mistake to take that job."

"I'm sure everything will work out," Jo Ella said, injecting a note of sympathetic patience into her voice. "But what I called about was this. I'd like to fix Cam something special for dinner tonight, and I don't really know what he likes. Could you give me some ideas?"

"Oh, what a nice thing to do," exclaimed Avis, pleased. "There's nothing my boys like better than a good meal at the end of the day. I worry about Cam, though—he never eats right. That's because he doesn't have anybody to take care of him, don't you know? But," she concluded in a satisfied tone, "I guess that's all changed, now that you're here."

Jo Ella's smile was a little weak. "Yes, ma'am." She was beginning to think she might have taken on more than she could handle, and she certainly didn't want Cam's mother to get the wrong impression. But it was only one dinner, after all. "Could you tell me what you think he might like?"

"Well...Cam's always been mighty partial to my fried chicken."

Great. Now they were getting somewhere. Jo Ella poised her pencil above the paper. "How do you make that?"

There was just the briefest surprised hesitation. "Why, you just fry it, that's all."

Jo Ella sighed. Obviously, this was not going to be as easy as she had supposed.

"WELL, I THINK you're crazy, man." Burt pried the top off his Styrofoam cup of coffee and tossed it in the general direction of the trash can. "You're setting yourself up for nothing but trouble."

"Hmm?" Cam had only been paying partial attention to his brother's conversation for the past ten minutes. In fact, he could not honestly say that he had been giving his full attention to anything that had gone on around him this morning, a fact that Burt had so far been polite enough not to point out to him. His absentmindedness had already cost Cam a complete overhaul on an engine that should have taken no more than ten minutes to repair, and that was chastisement enough. Now Cam dragged his mind forward to focus on Burt, and he looked up. "What?"

They were having lunch in the office. "Office," of course, was a generous term when applied to the eight-by-ten storeroom off an even smaller official reception area. This was where the business had gotten started, before they could afford the luxury of the carpeted reception room in front of it or the spacious hangar behind it, and the room still showed its origins. The same old weather-scarred desk that Burt had rescued from a school auction, the squeaky oak pedestal chair with the seat worn down from so many generations of use that a perfect dip had formed in the middle, bleached out and shiny. Scratched and dented gray file cabinets, calendars from the past five years hanging precariously on the walls, cardboard boxes of old records—it was a storage place for everything from old tires to office supplies, and it smelled comfortably of motor oil and dust. Cam liked this room. It was a familiar link with where they had come from, like an attic in an old house. It held dreams for the future that now were only pieces of their past, and there was a good, solid feeling within its walls. Continuity and security.

Burt and Cam rarely had lunch together. Cam usually ate in one of the airport cafeterias, or if he had the time and was feeling adventurous, he drove down the highway for a hamburger or a taco. If Burt wasn't flying, sometimes he joined him, but not often. Today, however, Burt had brought sandwiches from the ham Mary had baked last night, he didn't have a flight until two, and even Cam's preoccupation did not keep him from one of Mary's baked hams.

Burt unwrapped one of the sandwiches and peered cautiously at the contents. "Damn," he said irritably. "She forgot the mustard again." He passed the sandwich to Cam. "How many times do I have to tell her—"

"She didn't forget," Cam told him patiently. "She just knows I don't like it. Here." Cam pushed aside the litter of papers on the desk and came up with a foil packet of mustard from one of the takeout restaurants he frequented.

Burt accepted it with a suspicious glance. "So how come you rate so high with my wife?"

Cam shrugged. "Mustard's easier to put on than take

off," he answered with his mouth half full, then swallowed and grinned. "Besides, it's a lot easier to get attention when you're a bachelor. Everyone feels sorry for you."

Burt made a disgruntled sound and began to squeeze the mustard on his bread. "Yeah, well, that ought to come to a screeching halt pretty soon," he said. "You're not exactly a bachelor anymore."

Cam took another bite out of his sandwich, not looking at his brother. "This is damn good," he said. "You're a lucky man."

Burt laughed shortly. "Yeah, if you had my bills and my worries and three screaming kids when you're trying to watch the Dodgers game, you'd think so." He took a bite out of the sandwich and capitulated after a moment. "She does cook a fair ham, though."

Cam smiled and reached for his own coffee cup.

They ate in silence for a while, then Burt, with his elbows resting on the desk and his second sandwich held in both hands just below the level of his chin, paused to give Cam a long, studying look. "You ain't fooling me, kid," he said quietly. "She's already got you tied up in knots. And it's only been two days."

Cam crumbled up the waxed paper that held the crusts of his bread and a few shreds of ham. He did not reach for another sandwich. He wasn't as hungry as he'd though he was. And his tone was much shorter than he had intended it to be. "Stay out of it, okay, Burt?"

"Sure, man, no problem." Burt's voice was thick with phony nonchalance. "You want to get your brains scrambled and your guts ripped out by a pair of tight jeans and a cute smile, hey, that's your problem, right? No business of mine."

Cam scowled at him, tossing the paper toward the trash can. "Right."

Burt put the sandwich down impatiently. "The hell it's not. You know what she did to you before. You were a damn mess for three months. She had your head so screwed up—"

"Just drop it, Burt," Cam said harshly, and thirty years of experience had taught Burt when to back off. He picked up his sandwich again.

Cam lit a cigar, drew on it for a while and tried to smooth out the angry lines on his brow. He did not like to argue with his brother. Especially when he knew Burt was right.

Cam picked up his coffee cup and sipped from it. "What happened before has nothing to do with now," he offered after a moment, as a way of apology. "We were kids then."

Burt continued eating and said nothing. But Cam knew that it had only been seven years ago and neither one of them had been kids.

Of course he was setting himself up for trouble. He had known it from the beginning, only it had been much easier to convince himself that he could handle it than to face the truth. And he hadn't expected it to get so complicated so quickly. He had made the move on Jo Ella last night; she hadn't come to him. He couldn't blame her for that. In all fairness, she had never come to him—not the first time, not this time. She hadn't called him. He had called her. She could have been in and out of Dallas in two days and their paths never needed to cross, but Cam couldn't leave well enough alone. He had to call her up, he had to invite her to move in, and he thought he could handle it. And for one and a half days he had done just fine.

He almost grunted out loud with amused derision at himself. That must be a new record. Jo Ella was a compulsion with him, like a dangerous drug that, once sampled, could not be put away. It didn't matter that he knew better, it didn't matter that he could see what it was doing to his life, it didn't matter that there was only one logical ending—because, just like a junkie, he always managed to convince himself that he could handle it. Lulling himself into a false sense of security while a time bomb ticked off inside his head. He knew better. But it just didn't seem to make any difference.

"So," Burt said casually after a time, "are you sleeping with her?"

Cam's eyes jerked in surprised anger to his brother's, then shifted away without further challenge. "No," he said simply.

"Great." Burt crumpled up his own wrappings, his appetite swiftly going the way of his brother's. "She's already done this to you and you haven't even gotten to the good part yet."

Cam smiled a little, briefly and shallowly, and dropped his eyes to the oily black liquid in his cup. Absently, he flicked ashes on the cement floor and let the cigar burn, forgotten, in his fingers.

The old pedestal chair gave a raucous squeak of protest as Burt leaned back in it, cradling his coffee cup against his chest, watching Cameron. "What did happen with you two before?" he asked after a moment.

"I never did know. One minute you were the hottest thing going and the next..." He made a snapping motion with his fingers, opening them on thin air. And that was just the way it had been.

Cam sipped the bitter coffee and forgot to grimace at the taste. "Nothing happened," he answered. "She just left."

Burt tried not to sound incredulous or disapproving. Communicating with Cam could be a very tricky business at times. "Just like that? No explanation, no nothing?"

Cam stared at his coffee again. "She got a job offer and moved on. Joey never stays anyplace long, you know that."

There were a dozen things Burt could have said; he wisely rejected most of them. But there was one thing he had to know. "And you just let her?" he insisted, baffled. "I mean, you were crazy about that woman—and you just let her walk away, just like that? You didn't try to stop her?"

Now Cam looked up, surprised. "Stop her?" He said the phrase with the same inflection he might have used to echo "murder her"—as though the concept was so outrageous it did not bear thinking about. And he shook his head a little, giving his brother a condescending glance. "You don't stop Jo Ella. She goes her own way when it's time to go, that's all." Just as she would this time, he could not forget that. She would be here one moment and gone the next, following the unpredictable currents that swept her in and out of his life, and there was nothing he could do about it. He should know that by now.

Burt's face twisted into a puzzled, disapproving little grimace, and he shook his head once, briefly. "I don't know, man. If it was me, and I was that torn up about a woman, I'd damn sure do *something* to stop her—or die trying."

Cameron smiled into his coffee cup. That was the difference between himself and his brother, he supposed. Burt charted his own course, and Cam didn't see the point in fighting head winds. "That's what makes the world go round," he said with a shrug.

"You know..." Burt reached inside the paper bag again, found another foil-wrapped package and drew it out. "Sometimes I think you and me, we just got ourselves a little mixed up when we picked out our women. We'd be better off trading." Cameron looked up curiously, but Burt was unwrapping the foil package on his desk. "Hey, oatmeal cookies. You want one?"

Cameron took a couple, though he really wasn't very interested, and Burt went on. "Mary's a nest builder, perfect for a guy like you who wants nothing more than to diaper the kids and tend the crabgrass." Burt shrugged. "I like a little more space, you know, excitement. Like Joey." He bit into a cookie, then glanced at his brother once, shrewdly. "I had a thing for her one time, did you know that?"

Cameron stopped with his cookie halfway to his mouth, staring at Burt. "Joey?"

Burt nodded. "In high school. Well, she was in high school. I was home on leave from the army. Remember that first summer?"

Cam nodded, keeping his face very blank. But his throat felt heavy, and it was hard to speak. "Did you..."

Burt gave an impatient hiss of dismissal and threw his brother an accusatory look. "What, are you kidding? You think I wouldn't have told you about that? You think I would've tried anything with the girl my kid brother was mooning over, even if she hadn't been just a kid herself?" Burt dropped his eyes, pulling the soft cookie in half between his slender fingers. "Anyway," he said, and broke the cookie into fourths, "it was pretty bad that summer, and I guess I just wanted you to know I know how you feel. Joey... She's like high-powered jet fuel, you know? Good for the short haul but quick to flame out. And she'll damn sure burn you if you get too close."

Cam absently swirled the edge of his cookie in his coffee cup, keeping his eyes on his brother. "Did she ever know... how you felt, I mean?"

For a moment Burt's smile was reflective, a little amused. "No," he said. And he shrugged, popping a piece of cookie into his mouth. "Not that it would have made any difference. She was a busy little girl back then, didn't have much time for falling in love." And he shot Cam a brief, perceptive look. "Guess she hasn't changed all that much. Anyway"—he shrugged—"I met Mary, and it hasn't been all that bad. I guess we balance each other out or something."

Cam looked at his coffee-soaked cookie and tossed it in the trash can. His cigar had gone out, so he tossed that out, too. Burt began to dispose of the trash on the desk. He offered Cam the last cookie, and when he refused, ate it himself. "It's just a damn shame," he said, just when Cam thought the conversation was ended, "to see her screw up your life now, right when you've got everything the way you want it. I mean, you're starting to build something good for yourself, you know where you want to go and what you want to do with your life, right? Joey can't be a part of that. She can't do anything but sidetrack you."

Cam got up and dropped his half-filled coffee cup in the trash can.

"Have you told her about the farm?" Burt asked.

Cam hesitated. "No," he said, and then added, "No reason to. Like you said, it has nothing to do with her."

Burt tried to look satisfied, but Cam could tell he was still concerned. He really wished Burt would stay out of this. It was the curse of having a big brother, he supposed.

Cam started to walk back to the hangar, and Burt called after him, "You going to stay and finish that engine tonight?"

Cam replied automatically, "No, I've got to get home." And before he turned he knew how Burt would react to that statement. Cam had never rushed out of the shop before. He made his own time and followed his own schedule, just as all bachelors did. And this just proved Burt was right to worry, because Cam wasn't thinking like a bachelor anymore.

Cam met the accusation and worried sympathy in his brother's eyes without flinching. "Joey's waiting for me," he said simply, and went back to work.

IT WAS ALMOST FIVE O'CLOCK when Jo Ella finally accepted defeat. The chicken was a crispy soot-color on the outside, red and greasy on the inside. The potatoes were watery, the biscuits rock hard. Flour was sprayed from one end of the kitchen to the other, grease was splattered on the stove and the wall behind it, and blobs of batter dotted the countertops and dripped on the floor. The sink was overflowing with dishes, and there was a charcoal odor in the air that threatened to make her failure a permanent part of the ventilation system. A flat blister was rising on her thumb, and flour handprints branded her jeans and her cheeks.

Jo Ella stood in the corner of the kitchen for a moment, arms crossed and foot tapping, scowling at the mess, which by now was obviously unsalvageable. She was remembering why her mother had said she was hopeless all those years ago, and she was glad that her self-esteem was not heavily invested in her domestic accomplishments. But she couldn't leave Cam's kitchen like this. And she refused, absolutely refused to be made a fool of by a barnyard fowl one-tenth her size and possessing less than a quarter of her intelligence.

It was ten minutes to six when Jo Ella placed a platter of the Colonel's finest on the table, lit the candles, and wiped the last of the flour from the countertops. She heard Cam's key in the lock and hurriedly stuffed the telltale takeout bag into the trash can under the sink, then went to greet him.

"I don't believe this," Cam said softly, staring at the candlelit table. And his eyes went to Jo Ella, softening with unmistakable pleasure even as he said, "Really, Joey, you didn't have to..."

"I wanted to," she insisted, dismissing it quickly before the admiration she saw in his eyes could start to work on her guilty conscience. "Come on, let's eat."

Jo Ella had thought she would be too tired to eat, but

once she was across the table from Cam her pleasure in the meal was almost as great as his. It was nice to sit down at the end of the day with the man she had been waiting for, to share a meal and conversation in the cozy intimacy of a home, to watch the movements of his hands and the changing expressions on his face and the light in his eyes and to be captured, fractionally, by the dazzling warmth of his smile. Why had Jo Ella never realized this before? Her life seemed so empty up until this moment, devoid of all the small pleasures she had never even imagined could exist.

This was dangerous, Cam knew. Just when he thought he had fortified himself against all of Jo Ella's appeals, she did something totally unexpected to turn his head around. She was making him think, once again, that there might be a chance for them. She seemed so content, so happy doing nothing but staying with him and taking care of him, that he was beginning to imagine it might be permanent. He was beginning to imagine that there might be possibilities he had only dreamed of before, and that, of course, was ultimately foolish. He knew Jo Ella better than anyone else in the world. He knew her and he accepted her just as she was and without embellishment. Whatever was going on with her now was nothing he could count upon, or hold on to, as much as he wanted it. Jo Ella would start to smother in this environment before too much longer, and anything he tried to do to make her stay would be selfish and cruel. He must remember that.

Jo Ella was aware that Cam had grown silent during the last part of the meal, and she wondered what he was thinking. That was foolish. He was thinking about last night, of course, just as she was. And the troubled frown that was barely shadowing his features was nothing more than worry about what he had gotten himself into. Cam was a man of strong feelings and a deep sense of honor, and it was only natural that he would feel sharing Jo Ella's bed while she was under his protection would be taking advantage of her. Jo Ella understood that, just as she knew that already he was giving her more than she deserved and she had no right to ask for more. But that did not make her need for him any less.

Cam helped her clear the table, and she was glad she had cleaned the kitchen before he got home. He brought in the dishes while she stood at the sink and rinsed and stacked them in the dishwasher, and every once in a while Jo Ella stole a glance at him. There was something intimate in the act of performing this domestic chore together, and somehow he looked even more endearing than ever with the open cuffs of his denim shirt folded back, plates and cups balanced in his hands, pushing open the café doors with his shoulder.

"Thanks again, Joey," he said with a smile as he brought the last of the dishes to her. "It was great."

She shrugged, quickly concentrating her attention on the platter she was rinsing. "It was nothing. I just wanted to make up a little for last night." She said it before she realized it, and then she stiffened. He did not want to talk about last night. How stupid could she be? Why did she have to bring that up?

Cam reached around her very carefully to set the dishes in the sink. His arm brushed her shoulder. And he said, measuring his words into studied mildness, "What about last night?"

Jo Ella reached forward slowly and turned off the taps with both hands. She could feel him standing close to her, his warmth washing over her, the clean fragrance of him enveloping her. *Cam never smelled like grease,* she remarked absently to herself, with a very faraway part of her brain, *always like fresh air.* And she could feel the little hairs on the backs of her arms standing up, he was so close.

She turned around to face him. He hadn't said a word, he had not even touched her, but her pulse was tingling and there was a warm, melting feeling just below her breastbone. His eyes were grave, mildly questioning, but otherwise politely detached. There was nothing threatening about him. He towered over her, and the breadth of his shoulders blocked the rest of the kitchen from her vision, but there was nothing intimidating about Cam—except that his mere presence drew her like a magnet, she could not pull her eyes away from the way the pale-blue material strained across his lean chest, and she had to close her fists to keep her hands from reaching up to caress his strong, bare throat. She felt the small of her back pressing into the edge of the sink, and she said quietly, "I'm sorry about last night, Cam. I had no right to—to come on to you like I did, and I know—"

Surprise flickered in his eyes, and confusion. He made an involuntary movement to touch her that was never completed. And then, as he looked at her, his face softened, puzzled regret shadowed his eyes, and he lifted his hand again to touch her hair lightly. "Joey," he said quietly, "don't apologize. I'm the one who behaved badly last night, and I'm the one who's sorry. The last thing I wanted to do was hurt you."

She looked at him, her eyes wide and vulnerable, trying to understand. The gentle movement of his fingers on her hair and the tenderness in his eyes were drawing her back to long-ago days, and it was very hard to understand anything. "It was good between us," she said unsteadily, holding his gaze.

She saw the tensing of the long muscle in his neck that reflected his slight catch of breath. His eyes dropped slowly, following the path of his cupped hand as it drifted over her cheek, around her ear, to her neck. He said in a low voice, "I know."

His thumb brushed her lower lip. Her lips parted automatically and he repeated the motion, slowly, deliberately. A web of loosely woven electricity began to form around them as his other hand came up with tender absorption to push her hair behind her ear, a forefinger tracing the shape of her eyebrow and outlining the shape of her eyes. Jo Ella felt the melting flush begin to tingle across her skin, starting with the touch of his fingers and gradually creeping throughout her body. Her breath was a warm knot in the middle of her chest, and her muscles, held so carefully stiff, began to loosen helplessly. Without volition, her hands lifted, resting for a moment against Cam's chest, then traveling slowly upward to his shoulders, feeling the rough material of his shirt give with her movements, feeling the tingling heat of slightly damp skin penetrate the fabric and seep into her fingertips.

Jo Ella watched Cam; Cam watched the movements of his own hands with intense, almost wondering absorption as they moved slowly over her body. He traced the sweep of her small shoulders, cupping her upper arms, and his touch was so light only the warmth of his fingers penetrated the sleeves of her shirt. The pressure of his hands did not touch her at all, but it seemed her skin expanded to reach him, melting into him. His fingertips explored the narrow triangle of flesh exposed by her open collar, and Jo Ella moved her hands to circle his neck, her thumbs braced against the pulse of the vein near his collarbone, fingers splayed over the rough, heated texture of his skin. She could not span the circumference.

Cam's hands moved downward, so lightly it seemed he barely brushed her clothing, as though he were tracing her shape in the air or reconstructing her from memory. Each movement was slow and deliberate, suspended and examined in time, a moment in which he continually rediscovered her, but which felt to Jo Ella more as though he were creating her, forming her from nothing and giving her substance with the touch of his fingers.

Cam's palms shadowed her breasts, a cupping motion that barely touched, and Jo Ella felt the surging pressure from within in which her flesh strained to meet his. Her heart throbbed and pulsed against the warmth of his hand as slowly, so slowly, his touch moved downward, tingling over her ribs, discovering the indentation of her waist, cupping the beginning of the swell of her hips, and there he stopped. His thumbs were braced lightly against her hipbones, his fingers spread over the small of her back, and he lifted his eyes to hers.

His eyes were dark, and sober, but there was a fever burning there. She could feel it in the moist flush that heated his skin and the pulse that throbbed so strongly beneath her thumbs, in the constriction of the muscles of his throat as he swallowed. She could feel it in the tension of his neck muscles and in the light, rapid fan of his breath across her cheek, and she wanted him, couldn't he see how much she wanted him? Now or forever, it didn't matter, just to be wrapped in his strong arms and sheltered by his body, to feel herself melt into him and become a part of him, to give herself over to his keeping.

But she saw the shadow come over his eyes, the gentle resolve that kindly but firmly pushed her away. Her arms were weak and aching and could no longer maintain their uplifted position. She let them slide slowly away, down the length of his chest, to rest at last limply at her sides. And she could no longer meet his eyes.

So much was the same, but so much was different. They were older now, and perhaps wiser. Cam saw that, even if she didn't. What had been between them before had been a fairy-tale love affair, which was the prerogative only of youth; it had been carefree and unfettered, and no doubt its very beauty had been enhanced by the passage of time. They could not recapture it. So much more was at stake now.

He had not asked her to stay, on that long ago morning when she had burst into the cramped storehouse that had served as his and Burt's first office. She had been so full of herself, so charged with excitement over the possibility of setting sail for unknown places as part of a ship's medical staff, that she had not even taken time to consider what this change of job would mean to her and Cam. When it struck her, with a visible shock, that following her dream would mean leaving Cam behind, he had stepped in immediately, full of congratulations and enthusiastic support. He had not once asked her to stay. She wondered what she would have done if he had asked, and she did not even know the answer to that.

"Oh, Cam," she said quietly, in a tired voice, and she could not even lift her eyes to his. "What happened to us? What did we do wrong?"

He was silent for a moment, and when he spoke his voice was filled with the same sadness that was slowly draining Jo Ella's energy and leaving her numb. "I don't know," he said. "Maybe we didn't try hard enough. Or maybe"—his hands slowly left her waist and dropped to his sides—"we tried too hard."

Then he stepped away from her and lifted his arm heavily to run his fingers through his hair. Just before he left the room, Jo Ella made herself look at him—and then she wished she hadn't. The sorrow on his face almost broke her heart.

Chapter Seven

"I don't see how you do it," Jo Ella said as Mary bent to tie her three-year-old's shoe for what must have been the third time in fifteen minutes.

She had finally accepted Mary's invitation to lunch, but the luncheon had been held at Mary's house because, in her advanced state of pregnancy, Burt did not like her to drive. Jo Ella did not try to argue medical facts against that kind of male logic, but she had offered to pick Mary up, rather than have her meet her at a restaurant, as they had originally planned. But Mary had insisted it was too much trouble to find a sitter for the boys and that she did not at all mind fixing lunch at her house.

The lunch itself had been quite nice—Mary was, naturally, an excellent cook—and the two preschoolers obligingly napped while their mother was entertaining her guest. Jo Ella had a feeling, generated by the sheer relief in Mary's eyes when minute after minute passed with no sounds from the children's room, that that sort of thing did not happen very often. And of course, the minute her eldest got home from school, chaos broke out again.

Mary straightened up with a tired smile, gave the little one a pat on his bottom that sent him scooting off and admitted, "Sometimes I don't know, either."

They had taken glasses of iced tea to the patio table, where Mary could more easily watch the sometimes murderous antics of her three offspring. The weather was still nice, and the sun was warm and dry on Jo Ella's shoulders. It would have been a very pleasant afternoon had the children been a little quieter and not quite so demanding.

Mary and Burt had a lovely home in one of the nice suburban areas of Dallas. The houses were still too close together for Jo Ella's taste, but they were all beautifully landscaped and designed. Mary had brought her home to its full potential with her excellent taste and perfect sense of color. The carpets were in cool pastels and the walls light and airy. Every piece of furniture, every knickknack and occasional table added to the effect of casual elegance. Each picture and mirror was carefully chosen for its enhancement of the scheme of each room, and the result was a picture-perfect portrayal of suburban comfort. Of course, everything was spotlessly clean, gleaming with wax and polish, not a coaster or an ashtray even a fraction of a millimeter off center, not a single streak on the floor-to-ceiling windows. Jo Ella had to ask whether Mary took care of the house by herself and was told that she did. Jo Ella was amazed.

Mary had her own sets of crystal, china and silver

subtly displayed in a cherrywood cabinet in the formal dining room. Jo Ella envied her that, and the realization surprised her. If truth be told, she would have to admit something very close to envy for everything about the house and Mary's environment—the settled-in feeling, the comfort and the security that came from knowing one belonged. This was Mary's home, Mary's children, Mary's husband. Mary knew exactly what her role was in life and she was adept at filling it. She had found her place.

In the two weeks that had passed since that second night at Cam's, Cam and Jo Ella had come to a semblance of a comfortable living arrangement. They were polite, companionable and, on the surface, perfectly at ease with each other. Jo Ella kept the tiny apartment neat and clean, and with the aid of the "gourmet dinners" section of the frozen-foods department in the local supermarket, she had an elegant meal waiting for Cam when he came home each night. The entire process took less than two hours out of her day. The remaining time Jo Ella spent by going on fruitless job interviews, running two miles a day, sunning herself on the balcony and listening to gossip of the increasingly enthralling adventures of the residents of the Colony from Cam's mother. She had to admit she was going a little stir-crazy, and it was probably desperation more than anything else that had prompted her to accept Mary's luncheon invitation.

Jo Ella knew she couldn't go on like this. Cam seemed to like having her around, he appeared to enjoy her company and was always very appreciative of the little things she did around the house, but Jo Ella could tell he was ill at ease, keyed up, and he kept a lot to himself. Sometimes she caught him looking at her with a disturbed, brooding frown hovering in his eyes, and it was always too quickly, too efficiently replaced with a smile when he knew he had been discovered. Jo Ella only wanted to make Cam happy, and she was not doing it. She wanted her presence in his house to be an asset, not a burden, but it wasn't working. And the process of trying was driving her crazy.

She knew she couldn't stay with Cam forever. Of course she would eventually have to move on; it just was not within the pattern of her life to stay in any one situation or environment for an extended period of time. And this particular environment would have her climbing the walls in no time flat, she knew that. She couldn't live a satisfied life keeping Cam's house and fixing his meals and waiting for him to come home at night; she had never tried to deceive herself into thinking she could. It was just that, for a time, it was nice to imagine it could work. It was just that she wanted to be with Cam, and she wanted it to last as long as possible.

Jo Ella looked at Mary and smiled, trying to distract herself from the troublesome direction of her thoughts. "I guess you want a girl this time, huh?" she said.

Mary shouted, "Michael, you put that stick down this minute, do you hear?" She smiled apologetically at Jo Ella and wearily rubbed the back of her neck. "To tell you the truth, I really don't care. A baby is a baby."

Jo Ella tried to hide her shock by taking a quick sip of her iced tea, but Mary's smile was dry. "I know, that sounds awful, doesn't it? It's just that . . ." She shrugged. "I don't know. I thought having kids and a husband and a home was what I wanted—and it's not that I regret it, exactly. I mean, I love my boys and I love Burt, and I know what I do for them is important—but it's so confining, you know?"

Jo Ella's smile was sympathetic but light. "You realize, of course," she said, "that what you have is a case of the ninth-month blues."

"Is that it?" Mary murmured absently, but her attention was on a fight that was developing across the lawn. She opened her mouth to intervene, but the boys settled it among themselves at the last minute. She sat back again.

Jo Ella inquired, "Did you ever work?"

"Oh sure." Mary laughed. "You are looking at the proud owner of a master's degree in engineering—which makes me only slightly overqualified for my present job. I worked the first year we were married," she explained, "then I got pregnant and..." She shrugged.

Now Jo Ella was really shocked, both because she had never guessed that Mary was so talented and because she was appalled at what could only be considered her present waste of that talent. "Burt wanted you to quit?" she ventured.

"Oh, no," Mary said quickly. "It was my decision. Sometimes," she continued reflectively, "I think Burt might even have liked it better if I had continued to work. But," she insisted, "raising children is an important job, and I decided to give it my best shot."

Jo Ella felt a sweep of admiration for the woman's courage and dedication that humbled her, but also a certain amount of confusion. Jo Ella did not know whether she could ever make that choice. "Then," inquired Jo Ella, "you've never considered going back to work?"

"No," Mary answered, "not until the children are all much older. I've sometimes considered," she joked, "just walking out and leaving the whole bunch without looking back—but as long as I'm here, I'm going to do the job right."

"I think that's incredible," Jo Ella murmured.

Mary lifted her shoulders. Jo Ella could not tell if the gesture was more one of light dismissal, or of shifting a heavy burden into a less uncomfortable position. "Sure, it sounds good in theory," Mary said. "It sounded terrific to me when I first made the decision. What I didn't realize, of course, was that the grandest schemes come complete with the best booby traps. The dullness. The restrictions. I mean, sometimes it seems like my whole life is circumscribed in a one-mile perimeter—from here to the grocery store to the elementary school and back. Once a week dinner with Burt's mom, and even that's a chore by the time we get the kids cleaned up to go over there and cleaned up to come back." She paused, grimacing a little as she shifted her weight more comfortably in the chair. "Sometimes I get so bored I could scream. Sometimes I think if I could just do something different—*anything*, just one day a week, even—I wouldn't have the urge to strangle those three quite so many times a day." Again she shrugged. "It's the thousand little tensions that make up an ordinary day that I never counted on. It wasn't the load of bricks that broke the camel's back, you know, it was the straw."

Jo Ella was at the same time both puzzled by Mary's

confession and in complete empathy with her sentiments. Mary had always seemed so content to Jo Ella, the Total Woman Jo Ella herself could never be, and she and Burt had the perfect upwardly mobile middle-class marriage. The cars, the house, the kids, all those things Jo Ella herself would never have room for—but nonetheless sometimes missed. On the other hand, it was a relief to realize that Mary was not Superwoman, that she was having troubles coping with the life-style that had always seemed so alien to Jo Ella, but that she was, in fact, managing. Everyone made compromises, Jo Ella supposed. Perhaps there was hope for her yet.

"Maybe," Jo Ella suggested, "it wouldn't be a bad idea for you to get out more. There's no law that says you absolutely have to spent every waking moment with your children, you know. In fact," she elaborated, for she had once taken a course on parenting that was a requirement for a job at a family health clinic, "children actually benefit from time apart from their mothers—it teaches them independence and self-reliance. You don't have to go back to work full-time, but isn't there some hobby you'd like to take up? A class or something that would get you out of the house a few hours a week?"

Mary glanced at her, a secretive, slightly self-effacing little smile curving her lips. "Do you know what I'd really like to do?" she said, and there was a sparkle in her eyes. Jo Ella realized, to her surprise, that that was the first time she had ever seen Mary's eyes sparkle. "Take flying lessons," she confessed.

Jo Ella laughed, delighted. "But that's perfect! Burt's a pilot, right, and he could—"

But Mary dismissed it with a wave of her hand. "Burt would only laugh. He never takes me seriously any more." At that point, a genuine free-for-all broke out in the front yard, and Mary pushed herself laboriously out of the chair to go referee.

When the fight dispersed with only one bloody nose and one scraped knee, both of which Jo Ella attended to with admirable aplomb, it was getting late, and Jo Ella decided she had better go if she wanted to have Cam's dinner ready on time. But before she left, Mary insisted that she take home a plant stand that Cam had expressed interest in but was always forgetting to pick up. They got the stand, a little dusty from its long hibernation in the garage, disassembled and packed into the back of Jo Ella's car. As she backed out of the driveway and gave them all a cheerful wave, Jo Ella was struck by the poignancy of the picture Mary made, standing there with three children clamoring for her attention and a fourth, yet to be born, already etching lines of weariness on her face. She looked rather forlorn as she watched Jo Ella drive away.

Later, Jo Ella would look back on that day and blame herself for all the things she had overlooked. The underlying threads of desperation, the mute cry for help, the hundred subtle little signals that she should have picked up on. Later she would look back and see all the things she should have done, or could have done, to make things different. But, of course, by then it was too late.

JO ELLA STOPPED on her way home and impulsively bought a collection of houseplants to go on the new stand, then spent almost an hour dusting and reassembling it, then arranging the plants in it before the balcony door. She was just stepping back to admire the effect when the phone rang.

It was her mother, and Jo Ella tried to greet her cheerfully while preparing for the inevitable reproaches and guilt-inducing questions: "Why haven't you called? We've been so worried about you. Do you have a job yet?"

But today her mother surprised her. She only said, "I just wanted to make sure you were planning to come down for Thanksgiving. We're expecting you to spend the weekend. Bobby and Cindy are driving down, but there's going to be plenty of room."

Jo Ella tried to keep her plummeting spirits from sounding in her voice. "Oh. The whole family is going to be there, huh?" Four brothers, two sisters, an assortment of wives, husbands and children—the Thanksgiving reunion at Jo Ella's house was more along the proportions of the Democratic National Convention than a simple family dinner.

Her mother sounded slightly insulted. "Naturally. They always are—everyone except you, that is. And since this year you're at least in the state, there's no reason you can't make it. You haven't even seen Ricky's youngest yet, have you? And Lord knows how long it's been since you and Sandi got together. It'll be just like old times," she finished, pleased at the prospect.

"But, Mom," Jo Ella protested, without much hope, "where are you going to put all those people?"

"We always make room," her mother returned

cheerfully. "I've already started baking my pies and cakes and putting them in the freezer, I've got two Butterball turkeys..."

Jo Ella listened to her mother ramble on about the grocery list for a moment, and though it shamed her, she was desperately trying to think of some way to get out of it.

She loved her family, but all of them together were a little hard to take, and this year would be especially bad.

"So, we'll see you sometime that Wednesday," her mother announced, abruptly putting a finish to the conversation, as she always did with long-distance calls. "Everything going all right with you?"

"Oh...yes," replied Jo Ella absently. There simply was no way to get out of it. None at all. "Just fine."

"Glad to hear it. Bring Cam if you want to," she added as an inspiration, as though sensing her daughter's reluctance.

"I'm sure Cam has plans with his own family...."

"Well, whatever," her mother replied, unconcerned. "See you in a couple of weeks."

Jo Ella put down the phone with a grimace of minor annoyance, but she knew she was really more irritated with her own reaction to her mother's phone call than with the call itself. She was twenty-seven years old, and by now she should be able to hold her own with her family. Why did she let things like this upset her so?

Cam came in, as scheduled, just as she was putting the finishing touches on the table. He looked at the plant stand and at the candlelit table, and he lifted an eyebrow. "Well, well," he said. He was smiling, but he looked tired. And his smile never seemed to reach his eyes anymore. "Has my little bird gone domestic on me?"

"Mary said you wanted the plant stand," Jo Ella replied, watching him carefully. "Don't you like it?"

"Sure, it looks fine." He came to the table casually, and still his smile seemed rather vague. "You didn't have to go to all that trouble, though—plants and everything. I would have done it."

More and more lately, Jo Ella had the feeling that nothing Cam said had anything at all to do with what he was thinking. He was upset about something—if such a strong word as "upset" could ever be used to describe his unerringly placid disposition—and it had nothing to do with plants. It was just another reflection of the strain that was between them constantly, the discontent they were each struggling to ignore and cover with careful courtesy.

Jo Ella brought two plates of perfectly prepared Stouffer's beef Stroganoff from the kitchen, and Cam held her chair for her as she sat down. That was when Jo Ella was struck, as she was every evening, by what was missing. Here was the cozy domestic scene, the man coming home after a hard day at the shop, the woman waiting for him after a busy day at home; the candles were lit and the dinner was prepared. This was the point where they should have kissed and held each other, and brought each other comfort for the hardships the long day apart had caused them. His eyes should have lit up at the sight of her, and her heart should have swelled when he walked in the door, and their separate burdens should have faded into the background of yet another day the moment they stepped into each other's arms. That was what coming home was all about.

But instead, they sat down at a mutual table and made conversational small talk, two strangers who happened to share a home—which, of course, was exactly what they were. Oh, yes, Jo Ella's heart filled when he walked in the door, and the evenings with him were the goal her days were directed toward, but Cam's eyes did not light up when he saw her. In fact, coming home only seemed to add to his strain.

Conversation was desultory over dinner, polite but distant. Jo Ella told him about her afternoon with Mary; Cam complimented her on the dinner and told her a little about his day at work. Then he said, "I've got tickets to the Western Jamboree Saturday. I thought you'd want to go."

"Oh, yes!" The Western Jamboree was an open-air concert by what the radio billed as "the biggest collection of country-western stars ever assembled," and of course Jo Ella wanted to go. It was the kind of thing she and Cam used to do together, and they always had such fun. "Only..." she lowered her eyes to her fork as she lifted a single noodle, hiding from him the trepidation that threatened to obscure her pleasure—"it's general admission seating, isn't it?"

"Yeah, it's going to be a mess, too. We'll have to get there sometime in the afternoon if we want a seat. The crowds..." Then Cam hesitated, understanding. "The crowds will be rough," he finished quietly. He lowered his fork and looked at her, nothing but gentleness in his eyes. "Do you want to pass on this one?"

The warmth that spread through Jo Ella was more

than for the thoughtfulness of the question—more, even, than gratitude for his understanding. It was the touching of a bond that she had thought was broken, the reminder of things she had forgotten. It was like stumbling around in the dark and suddenly feeling the steadying handclasp of a friend. She did not have to explain to Cam; he knew.

"No." She smiled. "I can handle it. In fact," and she really meant it—"I wouldn't miss it for the world!"

Cam relaxed, and for the first time in weeks Jo Ella felt, rather than simply saw, his smile.

"My mother called today," she told him as they cleared the table.

"Thanksgiving, right?"

Jo Ella nodded, again grateful for his quick grasp of all the things that bothered her. No one else in the world knew her as well as Cam; why had she never realized before what a valuable characteristic that was? Silent understanding, instant empathy—how rare it was to have someone in your life, just one person, to whom you never had to explain anything. Who simply knew, without being told, how it was with you. How could she have taken it for granted for so many years?

"Everyone's coming." She could not keep the glumness out of her voice as she opened the dishwasher. "Talk about your crowds..." She began to stack the glasses in the top rack, shrugging a little. "It's not that I don't like to see them all, but you know how it is. 'Why isn't Jo Ella married by now?'" she mimicked gossiping relatives. "'Is Jo Ella still gallivanting around the world?' 'Isn't she ever going to settle down?' 'Don't you have a young man, Jo Ella?' 'You really should buy a house, Jo Ella?'" She stacked the last dish and closed the dishwasher with a little more vehemence than necessary. "Everyone with their babies and their new cars and their vacation stories. It's terrible to say," she admitted, "but I really don't have much in common with my family anymore. I just don't belong there, and I always feel like these family gatherings are just an excuse for taking potshots at Jo Ella."

Cameron let a short, dry smile of agreement play over his lips as he leaned casually against the counter, listening to her. "And," he pointed out seriously, "this year is going to be worse than most."

As always, he went straight to the heart of the matter without Jo Ella's having to bring it up. In previous years, Jo Ella might have been the target for innocent family gossip and speculation, but the events of the past months could not help but bring out the worst in people. Not malice, certainly, for Jo Ella's family was basically a close-knit, loyal structure, but morbid curiosity, unpalatable sympathy, endless pats on the shoulder and constant offers of helping hands. Jo Ella merely nodded bleakly.

Cam said thoughtfully, "You can't exactly just refuse to come."

Jo Ella laughed rather wryly. "Hardly. I mean, I've gotten out of it for the past four years, but I can't plead being on duty or on the other side of the world this year." She finished wiping the counters, rinsed the sponge and squeezed it dry with a rather vicious motion, then she squared her shoulders against the inevitable and allowed her face to fall into lines of resignation. She was ashamed of herself for making such a big deal out of it, and for resenting the family whose only crime was to love her and be concerned about her. "I'll live," she said, somewhat apologetically.

"Guess you'd better," Cam agreed, and turned to go into the other room. "Looks like this is one you're just going to have to get through."

Why did that sound like desertion to Jo Ella?

When she came into the living room, Cam was on the phone with his mother, Jo Ella's problems completely forgotten. She tried not to be hurt over that. It was just another sign of the buffer space he had thrown up between them, a sort of demilitarized zone that allowed them to just touch the boundaries of closeness but warned against dire consequences should they ever cross over that invisible line. Cam was very diligent about protecting those borders.

Jo Ella knew he was talking to his mother by the long listening periods in which he merely nodded sympathetically or murmured an understanding "Hmm." Every once in a while he would interject "Now who is Tracey again?" or "And what did Lewis do?" and Jo Ella knew Avis had launched again into one of her spiels of gossip about the dramas in the neighborhood.

"Well, Ma," Cam said at last, obviously desiring to put an end to the conversation, "it seems to me that if it's his baby he's got a right to know about it. . . ." Jo Ella lifted an eyebrow. Obviously, things were getting pretty racy over in the Colony. She would have to remember to call Avis tomorrow and find out the details. Cam sighed. "Yeah, I know, but . . ." A pause, and Jo Ella strained to make out the details of Avis's end of the conversation. "Well, I don't know what Beatrice is going to do," Cam said when he could get a word in, obviously growing a trifle impatient with affairs that really didn't concern him, "but I'm sure they'll work it out. Meanwhile, you try not to worry about it, okay? Listen, what I called about—"

Another interruption, and Jo Ella stifled a giggle at Cam's look of intense forbearance. Finally he said, "Well, that's fine, Ma. Whatever you think." Then, "Listen, what I called about was Thanksgiving. What do you think about doing our thing in Lubbock this year, with Joey's folks? You know, like we used to."

Jo Ella stared at him, hardly believing it. He was doodling absently on the telephone pad, not looking at her, his expression very casual. "Sure," he said, "why don't you give her a call? It'll save work all around, seems to me.... Yeah. Yeah, I'm sure she will. Sounds great. Why don't you just call Joey tomorrow and let her know what you've worked out? Okay, great. Talk to you later, Ma."

He hung up the phone and glanced at Jo Ella nonchalantly. "I thought it might be easier for you," he explained, "if you had a little moral support. Besides, if Burt flies us down, you'll only have to stay the one afternoon."

Jo Ella could restrain herself no longer. With a cry of sheer gratitude, she flung herself on the sofa and wrapped her arms around him, hugging him hard. "You're wonderful, wonderful, *wonderful*!" she exclaimed, laughing and punctuating each "wonderful" with a playful, childlike kiss on his chest and shoulders. Cam hugged her back, laughing with surprise and delight, and years melted away as they wrestled together with the unrestrained enthusiasm and open affection of the children they once had been.

It was only natural that the playfulness between them should blossom slowly into passion. The barriers were down, instinct dictated that they step forward. For the first time in her recent relationship with Cam, Jo Ella felt the rightness of it, the ease of it, and she welcomed it joyfully without even giving a deliberately, conscious thought to what was happening. She felt Cam's fingers tighten on her back, his warm breath on her neck. She let herself move against him, her breasts pressing into his chest, and his lips touched her neck, just above her collarbone. A shiver of pleasure tingled through her, and she caught her breath as his hands slid downward, his thumbs tracing the indentation of her waist, and she felt the touch of his tongue on her skin.

It was so easy, so lovely, to be carried way mindlessly into something that had belonged to them always. Jo Ella forgot the strain that had been between them, she forgot the rejection and the sorrow and the caution that had been so often in his eyes, she knew only that it was Cam, and it was she, sharing feelings that had never died, moving inexorably toward the wonder that had always been theirs.... And then Cam braced his hands against her waist, lifted his face from her neck; he very calmly and deliberately moved away.

It hurt more this time than it ever had. It felt like a heavy weight landing solidly in the middle of her stomach; a punch coming out of nowhere to knock her breath away. The pain and the shock of it welled up in her eyes, and she could only stare at him.

Cam's face was so expressionless it could have been a wax mask. His voice was so casual that the events of a moment ago could have been entirely within Jo Ella's imagination. He felt nothing at all, he was emotionless, a robot—and he did not want her.

"Burt said something about playing poker tonight," he said easily, drawing a cigar from his pocket. There was absolutely nothing in his eyes. "Do you want to go?"

They had to talk about this, Jo Ella knew. They could not go on like this. But something within her made her try to play his game just a little while longer. Maybe it was no more than just automatic words bypassing a numbed and reeling mind. "No." It surprised her that her tone almost matched, note for note, the nonchalance in his. Her fists closed on her thighs. "Not tonight. Thanks anyway. You go ahead though," she urged. Was that what he wanted, then? Freedom? Was she making too many demands on his time, closing in too tightly on his life-style? Then why didn't he *say* so? Why did he simply continue to look at her with those distant, blank eyes as though she were just another fish in his aquarium, interesting to watch but of no real consequence to him? Jo Ella didn't know. She couldn't tell what Cam was thinking anymore, and her head spun and ached from trying.

He held the cigar lightly between his fingers, stroking it, just watching her. "No," he said. "You were the only one who could ever give Burt any real competition." He was still talking easily, as though this conversation were the most natural thing in the world and nothing had preceded it or was likely to follow it. Jo

Ella thought she was the only one who could feel the tension that hovered over them, descending toward them and beginning to wrap itself around them like a summer storm cloud ready to burst. "I guess I just don't have that competitive spirit," he continued. "Burt says I always fold too soon. But you and he, though, are a perfect match, a fight to the death. I think the only reason he mentioned the game was to try to get you to come."

Jo Ella took a breath that did not ease in the slightest the aching in her chest. Why was he doing this? Why was he rambling on about poker games and Burt when he must surely see she was ready to scream with frustration and confusion. She said, "I'm really not up to an all-night game tonight. Maybe another time."

"You're not really up to too much lately, are you?" Cam murmured, and he reached for the lighter on the table. But before Jo Ella could respond, or even think of a response to that, he glanced at her and said, "Did you know Burt was in love with you once?"

Once again she felt that weighted feeling pounding into her stomach, and Jo Ella stared at him, her jaw dropping in an astonished gasp. "*What*?" she croaked, when a heartbeat's time had restored her breath. "Burt?"

There might have been a flicker of something in Cam's eyes—relief or satisfaction—but it was gone quickly as he brought the flame to his cigar, and he said nothing.

Jo Ella gave only cursory attention to his revelation and its significance. She had never thought of Burt as anything other than Cam's brother, and whatever infatuation he might once have had for her was long since gone; she couldn't care less. What she did care about was what Cam was thinking, how he was feeling, and why he had brought it up at all. "Cam..." she said carefully, and her voice was a little hoarse. "Is—is that what's bothering you? Are you—jealous?"

Cam puffed negligently on his cigar, and if anything crossed his eyes it could have been a spark of careless derision. "What's there to be jealous of?" was all he said, and Jo Ella could not even be relieved. Did he mean that he knew there had never been anything between her and Burt, or that he didn't care? Or perhaps both?

Jo Ella linked her hands tightly atop her jeaned legs, lowering her eyes to study with absent fascination the entwined pattern of her fingers. Something had to be said—she couldn't go on with all this confusion and hurt trapped inside her, carefully tiptoeing around Cam's boundaries and not knowing why. It shouldn't be like this between them. They shouldn't have unspoken restrictions tying them down, boxing them in. Jo Ella just couldn't go on like this much longer—and why wouldn't Cam talk to her?

"So," he said after another moment of thick, smothering tension between them, "How's the job search going?"

"Mrs. Bernell called this morning," she responded automatically, "about a medical secretary's job." Why was she letting him do this to her? She didn't want to talk about jobs and the lack of same—or was this the crux of the whole problem? Was it a gentle hint that her welcome here was wearing thin? *Why didn't he say what he meant?*

Cam lifted an interested eyebrow. "Sounds promising."

She laughed shortly, running a nervous hand through her tousled hair. "Can you see me stuck in an office for nine hours a day transcribing medical dictation? Come on!"

"No," he admitted thoughtfully. "But then"—he looked at her—"I never thought I'd see you do the kind of things you've been doing around here lately, either. At least, if you tied yourself down to a desk, you'd be doing it for money."

And there it was, the final confrontation. It could be postponed no longer. "Is that it, Cam?" she demanded quietly. "Do you want me to leave? To stop spending your money, stop hanging around your place, stop interfering in your life? Because all you have to do is—"

Cam interrupted patiently. "Joey, I told you before—"

"Then what?" she burst out, and anxiety combined with long-pent-up frustration caught in her voice like an angry sob. She felt color rising to her cheeks, and her eyes glittered. Her hands tightened again into fists on her legs. "You keep looking at me with that cold, hateful stare—you barely tolerate me here, Cam! Oh, you're always polite, always very gracious, but you don't mean it, you can't mean it—"

"Damn it, Joey—" He stabbed out the cigar with a vicious motion. "Let's not go through all this again." The line of his jaw was very hard, but he did not look at her. His voice sounded calm following the near-hysteria in hers. "You *are* welcome here, as long as you want to stay, I wouldn't have said that if I didn't mean it. It has nothing to do with—"

She interrupted him. "That's right, it doesn't." Her voice was tight, revealing the effort it took for her to try to match his even tone. "It has to do with me, something about me...." She had to stop for a calming breath, tilting her head against the tension that was knotting in her neck, fixing her eyes helplessly on the ceiling for a moment. "It never used to be like this between us," she said softly, measuring her words. "What am I doing wrong?"

Cam stood up abruptly, moving a few steps across the room. "Things have changed, Joey. We've changed. And you—you don't know what you want, any more than you ever did."

"That's not true, Cam," she protested, the words tumbling forth impulsively before she could stop them or analyze them. "I know what I want! I want—"

The word "you" was rushing to be spoken, and he would not give it a chance to reach her lips. He turned shortly, and the tight anger drawn into the lines around his lips, the repressed glint in his eyes, silenced Jo Ella. She had never seen Cam angry before. "Damn it, Joey," he burst out, "don't you know what it does to me to see you like this? Don't you realize what you're doing to yourself? Keeping my house, fixing my meals, being the perfect domesticated woman—"

Jo Ella was too shocked by his outburst to do more than stammer, "I—I thought you appreciated it. I only did it to—"

"To pay back some imaginary debt you think you owe me for letting you stay here," he returned curtly.

"I know that. Well, thank you very much, but I don't need your carefully cultivated talents around the house, and I won't have you making yourself into something you're not, for my sake."

"You're mad at me because I clean your house and cook your meals?" Jo Ella demanded incredulously.

Cam wrestled with brief frustration and indecision. "Yes. No. For God's sake, Joey, why don't you listen to me? I don't want you to change for me, I don't want—"

But Jo Ella could not listen to this nonsense anymore. She let a short breath hiss through her teeth, then got up and stalked to the kitchen. She returned in just a moment with an empty frozen dinner package, her eyes smoldering, her color high. "*This*," she declared, waving it at him, "is the extent of my domestic accomplishments! Any more complaints?"

Cameron looked at her and at the evidence of her innocent deception, and a rueful, defeated smile crossed his eyes. "I know you can't cook, Joey," he said tiredly, with a trace of apology in his tone. "That's not what this is all about, darling." He took the package from her and dropped it to the floor, then he placed both hands gently on her shoulders, closing the distance between them until their bodies almost brushed. And all Jo Ella could think was, *Darling. He called me darling.*

But his eyes were very serious now, and his tone was pained. "It's about compromises and obligations, and going through the motions; it's about the things we want from each other that we can't give."

She saw the sorrow in his eyes, and it tore at her

because she did not understand it. She wanted to scream with not understanding. She rested her hands on his forearms and thought if only he would close that embrace, if only he would stop being so noble and stubborn and careful everything would be all right. She wanted to shake him, she wanted to yell at him and curse at him and force some emotion from him, but her voice was very quiet, constricted by some pressure deep in her throat as she looked up at him and said simply, "No, it's not, Cam. It's about why you flinch every time I touch you. It's about why you push me away every time I try to get close and why you don't want me anymore. . . ."

And yet, with those softly spoken words that trailed off helplessly at the end, with the gravity of her expression and the helplessness in her eyes, she seemed to have stirred more emotion in him than any amount of violence could have done. She saw a low flame kindle far back in his eyes that was not pleasant, she saw the flexing of his jaw muscles and the tightening of his lips, all coming upon him gradually, as though he were fighting the anger and losing. There was desperation in his eyes, frustration and denial, and—the most alien emotion of all—defiance. His fingers closed around her wrist, hard. "It's not," he said roughly, pulling her hand down his body, across his arm and his chest, the leather of his belt and the scratchy texture of his jeans, "because I don't want you." He pressed her palm against his pelvis without gentleness; she felt the heat and the hardness and the strength of his erection, but it was such a hateful, spiteful gesture that she jerked her hand away with a gasp, taking a step back from him.

"Isn't that it, Jo Ella?" he bit out shortly. "Isn't that what you wanted to know?" Quick tears of anger and insult burned behind Jo Ella's eyes, leaving her speechless, and with a disgusted hiss of breath, Cameron turned away.

He ran his fingers through his hair in a tight gesture of bitter control, and when next he spoke he managed to keep most of the venom out of his tone. But it was still there, seething beneath the surface. "Damn it, Jo Ella, don't you see what you're doing? Don't you think I see? You've been doing it all your life—paying off debts before they can accumulate to tie you down. That's why you resented every kindness your mother ever did you, that's why you avoid a family who loves you. Hell, that's why you went into nursing, to do more good deeds than anyone else so no one could ever say you 'owed' them kindness. You won't let anyone give you anything without obligation because that's a sign of love and love is a trap. You won't be tied down by unpaid debts. So you've been bartering with me ever since you got here, with candlelight dinners and sparkling windows and witty conversation—even sex. Anything to make sure you don't owe me anything when you leave... even score, clean slate, no ties to bind you to me."

Jo Ella's breath left her body with an audible sound, and rage and disbelief swelled up in its stead. For a moment she was so hurt and so angry that she could not even speak; she was actually shaking. If Cam had been two steps closer she would have hit him; her arm even drew back to do it, but fury numbed her and she couldn't move. "How—how *dare* you!" she choked out hoarsely, at last. "How dare you imply that I would bargain my body for—for a place to stay, for—for... how could you say..." The words were growing incoherent, and gradually she realized that it was because tears were thickening her mouth and closing up her throat. "I never expected—you to..." No, she had never expected it, not from Cam, and the sensation was like a hot knife that seared through her body from throat to solar plexus, severing arteries and leaving nerve endings loose, dangling, exposed while the life seeped out of her with exquisite slowness and all possible agony.

Cam's face, when he turned, was shocked, as though he had only just heard his own words and could not believe he had said them. And then his eyes quickly filled with a reflection of Jo Ella's pain and he took a step toward her, his hand half lifted to touch her, but she turned away.

Jo Ella sank to the sofa simply because her knees were trembling too much to support her any longer. But she stiffened her back and kept her head up and refused to cry. Then she felt Cam sit beside her; his hand touched her shoulder.

"Joey..." he said. His voice was soft and filled with pain and confusion. "Honey, I didn't mean that the way it sounded. I didn't mean to hurt you...." And then he sighed; his hand dropped slowly from her shoulder. She felt the shifting of sofa cushions as he leaned his head back in a heavy gesture of defeat. "God," he said. His voice was low and bleak. "I can't believe what I just did. I can't believe I was fighting with you."

Jo Ella swallowed hard, stretching her throat muscles, trying to clear her voice for speech. She knew he hadn't meant it—or if he had, he had not meant it in a hurtful way. It was not the words themselves that hurt her, but the reason for them, the things he had left unsaid. It was knowing there was something hurting Cam and not being able to do anything about it. Not even understanding what it was.

For the longest time, the silence was broken only by the bubbling of the aquarium, the hum of the dishwasher in its rinse cycle and the sound of her own breathing. Cam was very still beside her. Jo Ella wanted to turn to him, to smile at him and somehow make everything normal again; she wanted to erase the past few minutes from history and start over again. But it wasn't finished. They both knew that.

"Joey," Cam began at last, quietly, "these past few weeks have been rough, for both of us. A lot of it's sexual, I know. We can't forget how easy it was before and we want it to be that way again. But it's not. At least not for me."

Jo Ella turned slowly to look at him. His expression was grave, his eyes troubled. He was asking her to understand but not expecting her to.

"I don't like what's been happening to us since you moved in," he said. His voice was heavy with sorrow, deep with concern. "I don't like the way you've been trying to change for me; I don't like the way I've been trying to get you to stay when I know the worst thing in the world I can do for you is to try to keep you caged up."

Jo Ella lay a hand atop his in instinctive protest, but

he shook his head before she could speak. "No, it's true. It was selfish of me to even ask you to come here, because I knew the first thing I was going to do was to try to find some way to get you to stay. But this is just a recovery period for you, Joey," he told her quietly. "You'll get your strength back, you'll get on your feet again—and you'll move on. You'll have to."

Part of her cried out in confused protest that that wasn't true, that it didn't have to be, that all she wanted to do was stay with him. But part of her accepted what he said because she was used to accepting what Cam said as unquestioned verity—because it had always been true. Why should things change between them now just because she wanted them to? Her heart was breaking for the sorrow in his eyes, and everything within her yearned and twisted with confusion and need, but in the end she had no defense to offer. None at all.

All she could say was, rather brokenly. "What do you want from me, Cam?" She would do anything, give anything, all he had to do was ask.

His smile was gentle, regretful and bleak. "More," he answered simply, "than just sex during intermission. I know that sounds rough, Joey, but we've got to face it. This is just a stopover for you, and I don't do well with short-term involvements. You don't know anything else. I'm who I am and you're who you are, and we can't do anything about that—except try not to hurt each other any more than we already have."

There was so much she wanted to say to him, so much she wanted to question and explain and plead... but it was all too new, too confusing, and she did not know where to begin. And before she could even get it sorted out in her mind, before she could think of a way to begin, he smiled, and his hand came up to curve around her neck. He leaned forward and kissed her gently on the forehead. "It'll be okay, Joey," he said softly, "as long as we don't try to change the status quo. You'll see."

And that was when Jo Ella realized that there really wasn't anything she could say. He had never asked for a commitment from her, and he wasn't doing so now. She could make no response because he had asked her no questions.

Nothing had changed, because Cam wanted it that way.

Chapter Eight

Jo Ella had not seen Burt since Cam had told her about the feelings he once had had for her, and she wondered if there would be any awkwardness. She was relieved when there was not.

Burt swung into the reception room with a cheerful "Hello, kiddo," and a wink. "You look mighty foxy this afternoon. How's it going?"

Jo Ella was wearing body-hugging jeans, knee-high leg warmers and a bulky rust-tone sweater, for although it was still warm in midafternoon, she imagined it would get pretty chilly at the concert tonight. She did not consider the outfit particularly "foxy," but she swept Burt a curtsy and responded, "Thank you, kind sir. So do you."

Burt grinned as he stopped by his secretary's desk for his messages. "Got to keep up the old image." Burt had always been a good-looking man, like his brother, but Jo Ella could not help thinking that Cam did not need a leather jacket and aviator glasses to make him look sexy. Burt was always terribly concerned with image.

He glanced through his messages, said a few words to the secretary, and then came over to Jo Ella. "Does Cam know you're here?"

She nodded. "He's changing." They had thought it would be easier if Jo Ella met him at the airport for the drive across town to the concert area. The traffic would be impossible in another hour.

The past week between them had been in some ways easier than any that had gone before. The fight between them, painful though it had been, had strangely seemed to clear the air—or perhaps it simply more clearly defined the boundaries that were off limits. Cam was more relaxed with her, and Jo Ella found it easier to accept his terms. Or at least she pretended it was easier, and during the daytime it was not so hard. It was at night, alone in her bed, that the doubts and the yearning began to assail her, and she lay awake for hours, aching for him and berating herself for it, trying to convince herself that he was right and she was wrong and that wishing for anything to be different was stupid and self-defeating. There were only two categories of things in this world: those she could have and those she could not. Why waste time mourning over the things she couldn't have when there was so much out there she could have? Only it wasn't quite that easy, because Jo Ella was having trouble figuring out what it was she did want, if she couldn't have Cam.

And she did not even allow herself to imagine what it was she wanted from him, what she would do if her wishes could come true. Because she knew Cam was right; he must be. There was no future for them, there never had been, and just because she came to him now, broken and hurting, was no indication that anything could be permanently changed. Maybe Cam was right, and she wasn't even sure she wanted permanence. Jo Ella did not know what she wanted. This need was too new, too tentative, to be fully analyzed, but she felt as though something was changing within her, or something long ignored was coming to life. This did not feel like anything she recognized about herself. This did not feel like something that would die when she got ready to move on.

And sometimes she had such vivid, erotic dreams about Cam that she was embarrassed to look at him the next morning.

Burt said, "So how's the job hunt going?"

That seemed to be standard conversational fare when anyone greeted Jo Ella these days, and she had learned not to resent it. After all, that was what she was supposed to be doing here; it seemed only logical that her primary interest, too, would be in the ups and downs of the job market. And she would not admit even to herself anymore that she had far more pressing concerns than unemployment on her mind. She shrugged. "Not so terrific. The jobs are out there, I guess, but nothing I'm qualified for."

Jo Ella had diligently increased her job-hunting efforts. She knew she had only been using Cam's protection, his generous offer of food and shelter, to avoid certain realities of a world that had suddenly turned harsh on her. And she knew that the sooner they ended their false domesticity, with all its illusionary qualities of comfort and home, the less painful it would be for both of them. About that, at least, Cam was right. But she routinely refused all job leads within the medical profession, and that narrowed the field of search considerably.

Burt frowned with concern. "That seems odd. I always thought you were one of the most qualified people in your profession."

"I'm getting out of medicine," Joe Ella explained to him. And for some reason she felt compelled to go on. "It was a decision I'd been putting off making, I think, even before this all happened with Bobby Williams." And she shook her head slowly. "I don't know. So much pain, so much dying, and there's so little we can do about it. It starts to get to you after a while, being helpless."

Burt nodded soberly. "Yeah, I guess I can see that. I sure couldn't handle it. Too much responsibility."

Jo Ella opened her mouth to protest, for the question of responsibility had never entered into the picture. But she said nothing because something about what he said disturbed her, more than she wanted to admit. Was there another reason, one she had not even had the courage to examine, for her suddenly deciding to sabotage her career?

Instead, she said brightly to Burt, "So how's the little mother?"

He grimaced. "Fat and lazy."

Jo Ella lifted an accusatory eyebrow. "Complaints, stud?"

Burt gave an abashed grin that let more than a little of his pride in impending fatherhood show through. "Who, me?" Then he added, "The doctor says she's doing good. We might even have a Thanksgiving baby."

"Think you might give up trying to populate the earth with little Scotts after this one?" Jo Ella teased.

Again Burt made a wry face. "It's not all glamour and glory," he agreed. "Sometimes I think you had the right idea all along, Joey. Cut your ties, just pick up and move on when things start getting too heavy. That's the way to live, all right. Don't hang around anyplace long enough to get bogged down. First thing you know you're falling in love, then you're making promises, then you're fluttering around on the ground with your wings clipped, and talk about your responsibilities..." He laughed a short, gruff laugh that was both self-derogatory and apologetic. "Oh, well. We make our own beds, don't we?" Then he winked at her, dismissing it. "And there *are* compensations."

Cam came in then with a cheerful "Ready to go?" and Jo Ella said goodbye to Burt rather absently. His words echoed in her mind, and they troubled her.

Cam looked particularly appealing tonight. His V-neck sweater was a pale teal color, and the denim jacket he tossed into the back seat was lined with sheepskin. He adjusted the seat on Jo Ella's car to accommodate his long legs and relaxed behind the wheel, leaning back, his slim brown hand guiding the steering wheel negligently. Cam never seemed to lose his tan. The deep cut of his sweater emphasized his strong neck and revealed a few inches of bare chest, and his hair was smooth and glossy as it drifted over his ears. Jo Ella thought, *There isn't a woman in the world who wouldn't want this man. Why should I be any different?* But Cam was very particular where he bestowed his affections.

Affections. That, of course, was the key word. Cam

made commitments, he did not have one-night stands. He was steady, reliable, even-tempered and never ruffled. It was not within Cam's life-style to go flitting from one love affair to the other without thought of permanence or emotional involvement—any more than it was within his personality to make impulsive decisions or take risks or seek a fight. Cam liked his life easy, predictable and secure. Unlike his brother, Cam welcomed responsibility.

And Jo Ella? All her life she had thought of herself as a capable, responsible person. Restlessness had nothing to do with it. She had taken responsibility for thousands of lives, hadn't she? She had cared for them and nurtured them, and when her work was finished she had moved on.

Or had she moved on only when, as Burt said, things became too heavy? When she started to care too much or become too involved, or when the burden of other people's suffering became too much for her to bear?

Cam said she had gone into nursing as a method of keeping some sort of psychological tally sheet balanced. That stung, but Jo Ella could not entirely deny it. Maybe he was right, maybe she did see the generosity and kindness of others as an obligation to be paid, and maybe the only way she could be free of it was to overcompensate by entering a profession that required constant self-sacrifice. But now—had it turned into a trap of her own making? Was her decision to leave nursing only another way of running away from the overwhelming responsibility?

She had been responsible for Bobby Williams. She had, for perhaps the first time in her life, completely taken the burden of another's suffering on herself. She had felt the weight of a human life, she had gotten involved, she had cared. And the experience had almost destroyed her.

She knew why Cam did not want her, why he could not afford to become any more involved with her. He understood, as Jo Ella was only beginning to, the real thing that was keeping them apart. It was her own limitations, boundaries she had imposed upon herself. She simply refused to take on the burden of another heart. She was afraid to accept the responsibility of loving him.

And that made her very sad.

BECAUSE IT WAS football season, the concert could not be held in one of the more adequate stadiums, as it might have been in the summertime. An open field on the outskirts of town had been set up with bleachers and a stage, and although it was still two hours before show time, the traffic was congested. They had parked in a lot six blocks away, and they weren't the only ones. It looked like a pilgrimage down every street surrounding the concert area, groups and lines of people laughing and talking and all heading in the same direction. Jo Ella felt her stomach began to tighten just imagining what the crowd inside the makeshift stadium would be like.

It was a pleasant day for a walk, the weather mild and the sky blue. Cam and Jo Ella joined the meandering streams of people who had arrived early for the best seats and walked at an even, unhurried pace toward the arena. This area of Dallas, like so many others, was under construction, and they had to be careful about broken sidewalks and overhanging scaffolding. The crowd had discovered a shortcut through a short stretch of open conduit that formed a tunnel from one street to the next, and with only a brief grimace of distaste, Jo Ella entered it with Cam. She wasn't crazy about tunnels, but it was short and sunlit and a few other couples were passing through with them. Their voices and laughter echoed cheerfully off the concrete walls.

When they emerged the crowd was thicker, all joining from different streets and moving in the same direction. There were college students handing out antinuclear fliers and vendors selling lemonade and Coke by the gallon—despite the fact that no containers of any sort were allowed behind the gates and guards were very dilligent about checking for thermoses, coolers and glass bottles.

They climbed a small incline and all of a sudden the concert area was in view. Jo Ella couldn't help tensing at the sight of all those people crammed together, milling on the sidewalks and in the streets, sitting on the grass, smoking, drinking, talking. Thousands of them. Multiple thousands, it seemed to her, a blend of colors and textures as far as the eye could see, so many, so close together, all of them shifting and moving and taking up air. Jo Ella could imagine herself being drawn down in that seething mass, being swallowed up and unable to escape, smothering....

Cam sensed her tension even before she spoke, and his hand came to rest lightly upon her back, a reassuring gesture like the one he might use to calm a skittish horse. And Jo Ella said quickly, tightly, "Cam, I don't think I can sit down there with all those people for two hours."

"I was just thinking the same thing myself," he responded easily, and his hand made long, soothing, stroking motions along her back. "What do you say we go get a hot dog or something? It'll be a long time before we get a chance to eat again."

The moment Jo Ella turned her back on the crowd she took a deep breath, and it wasn't until then that she realized she had hardly been breathing at all. The coolness she felt on her face was from drying perspiration, and she could still feel the fine, high quivering deep within her muscles like an electric wire on overload. She was embarrassed. Usually she could deal with her claustrophobia if she just plunged right in and didn't think about the crowds, if she put her guard up and made a constant, unwavering effort to ignore it, but that moment of standing on top of the hill and looking down had caught her off guard. She had panicked, and it was stupid.

She cast a quick, shy and apologetic glance at Cam, almost as filled with shame for her uncalled-for reaction as she was with gratitude for his smooth rescue. He must think she was an idiot. But Cam's face was relaxed and unconcerned, as though he saw nothing unusual at all about the episode. As though he hadn't even noticed it. Jo Ella let the last of the tension seep from her into patent relief.

They went into a small hot dog stand across the street that wasn't too crowded because most people were ordering food to go and taking it back to the gates with them. The outside of the place was battered and uninviting, the paint was peeling and the sign was leaning. The inside wasn't much better. Of the six vinyl booths, only one did not have stuffing spilling through the fabric, and that one was missing its back. The tables and floor were littered with paper napkins and food containers, and flies buzzed happily in and out. The floor itself looked greasy enough to skate on, and the man behind the counter looked as if he might have once been an army cook—and hadn't changed his apron since the last war.

Cam gave her an amused, skeptical look. "Well, Miss Health Inspector?"

"Are you kidding? she scoffed. "Anybody knows you can't get a good chili dog in a place that has clean windows. They spend all their time washing windows, who has time to cook, right?"

Cam laughed and they went inside.

What it lacked in hygiene, the place did, indeed, make up for in taste. The chili was thick and spicy, the melted cheese sharp and bubbly. The hot dogs themselves were plump, juicy and perfect, and the french fries so light they practically melted in her mouth. The root beer was on tap, and Jo Ella had two glasses. Sitting across that dirty little table from Cam, laughing with him and gorging herself while he teased her about her appetite and deftly downed three hot dogs himself, Jo Ella was reminded of their high-school days. They had had such good times then, she and Cam. Such innocent, carefree, purely happy times. She was always getting into scrapes, and Cam was always rescuing her. He was always there to help her cram for a test or to tutor her through geometry or to save her from dying of embarrassment when she had had a fight with her current boyfriend the night before and didn't have a date for the Best Party of the Year. Everyone envied her when she showed up with Cam on her arm at a dance or a football game—he was an older man, and so sexy, and no girl could ever pin him down. And when he was with Jo Ella he went out of his way to make sure she was envied, playing the game designed to bring her latest rejected suitor to his knees with jealousy or to humble the heart of a girl friend who had offended Jo Ella with some catty remark. He always gave her exactly what she needed, and he did it so naturally, so easily, that Jo Ella had never thought twice about it. He seemed to enjoy it, as though his happiest moments were in doing something for Jo Ella.

And here they were ten years later, having come full circle, laughing and eating hot dogs in some greasy-spoon diner, and Cam was still making her happy. Still taking care of her. Could they have imagined it, all those years ago? Jo Ella tried to think back to how they had been then, what their dreams had been, how they had thought. She did not think that either of them, at ages seventeen and twenty, had been gifted with any particular insight into the future, but it simply seemed as though she and Cam had always been together, and always would be.

"You know," she said thoughtfully now, "it's a pretty rare thing—to have a friend who's been around as long as you have. To know somebody all your life, to grow up with them, and to still share adulthood with them—I don't think that happens very often."

Cam nodded and smiled. "All the more reason to

treasure it," he agreed. "And to guard it very carefully."

Was that what he was doing now, Jo Ella wondered, and for just a moment a shadow passed over the contentment she had felt these past few minutes with him. Was that why he was establishing the rules and drawing the boundaries, to protect the friendship they had shared for over twenty years from further damage at Jo Ella's careless hands? Cam, the builder and the protector. He would know what was right.

Jo Ella was prepared for it this time, and she only felt a twinge of breathlessness before they were part of the crowd that covered the field, and then she didn't think about it anymore. They picked their way carefully over bodies who had staked their territory with stadium blankets and lawn chairs, but it was still early and there were a few good spots left. Some of the more prudent patrons had chosen to sit in the bleachers, but most were heading for the center-field, stage-front positions. Cam did not have any trouble finding a place for them—it was instinctive with most people to make way for a man of his size—and they sat on the grass directly in front of the stage and about fifty yards back.

Jo Ella noticed that the stage was surrounded by what appeared to her to be a tall fence of almost transparent chicken wire, and she pointed it out to Cam, puzzled. He laughed, his eyes crinkling into those familiar little lines that made Jo Ella want to touch him, and he said, "It's obvious you haven't been to one of these concerts in a few years."

She shrugged and admitted she hadn't. "This," Cam explained to her, glancing around him, "is what is called an earth-doggers crowd—good old boys who like to kick up their heels a little bit to the sound of country music. They can get pretty wild sometimes, and no matter how carefully the guards check for throwable objects, some jerk is going to sneak a beer bottle in and toss it at the stage in a burst of enthusiasm. The managers have learned a little chicken wire can prevent a lot of damage to their equipment—and their musicians. It's the same with punk rockers," he added. "Something about music in the open air just makes people go a little crazy."

Jo Ella looked incredulously from him to the stage and then back again. She shook her head sadly. "Now that," she said, "is a shame. When musicians have to perform in a cage."

"Sign of the times, sweetheart." He smiled, and then he reached forward and smoothed a strand of hair behind Jo Ella's ear. "You look awfully pretty tonight," he said softly.

There was no more than that—a gentle touch, a tender look and a simple compliment—but Jo Ella felt the world shift on its axis and the twilight brighten and begin to glow, and everything within her tingled in response. She could not remeber the last time she had blushed, but she blushed then. Cam noticed it, and his eyes twinkled. "That," he said, running a forefinger across her warm cheek, "is even nicer."

He settled back, leaning his weight on one arm close to Jo Ella's back, offering her the shelter of his shoulder. They sat together and watched the crowd, laughing softly as one successful-looking, clean-cut young man in a studded jacket and custom-designed cowboy boots made his way casually through the masses, offering an assortment of recreational drugs for sale. For a while it wasn't too crowded. There were people on all sides, but a space of a few yards remained between each group. Gradually, however, as newcomers arrived, personal space was decreased, and they were sitting almost shoulder to shoulder, foot to back with strangers. When Jo Ella made the mistake of tucking her legs under her, someone immediately plopped down in the space she had just vacated and Cam only gave her a wry look.

Behind her, a young boy was trying to pick up a girl next to him. Through the ebb and flow of dozens of conversations all around her, Jo Ella could not help but focus her attention on this one—he was practically speaking right into her ear.

The girl, Jo Ella had noticed previously, was a college student, and she had brought a textbook with her to study while passing time. Having failed with such old standbys as "You live around here?" and "Hey, you got really neat-looking legs, man"—Jo Ella almost choked on that one—the boy apparently decided on the intellectual approach, and he said, "Whatcha reading?"

The girl murmured something about a psychology text.

"Psychology, hey, wow, that's really heavy, man. I mean, that's really neat, the mind and all. I'm kinda interested in that scene myself. You mind if I look at it?"

Apparently the girl had no choice, for the next comment was, "heavy, man, really heavy. Look at all those damn monkeys and stuff. Where d'you go to school?"

The girl told him, which was probably her first mistake, for he took that as a sign of encouragement. "I'm a freshman at State. It's a real trip, man. I mean, I didn't think I'd really dig this college scene, but it's okay, plenty of action. I don't know if I'll keep it up, though. I mean, I figure life's too short, you know? I don't even know who I am or what I want to do and why am I tying myself down to some stupid school, you know? And some of them professors, you know, are like, really heavy...."

"Good God," Jo Ella groaned. She leaned closer to Cam and murmured, "Listen to that conversation behind us and then let's have a debate on the value of the public education system."

Cam nodded imperceptibly. "I know. He's got an earring and a Mohawk haircut. Real cool dude, man, I mean like, heavy..." he mimicked, and Jo Ella doubled over with repressed giggles.

"I didn't think people talked like that anymore," she whispered, still laughing. "Was that the way we used to sound?"

"God, I hope not," Cam murmured, still watching the boy with the earring. "I guess teenage intellect has no generation gap. The more things change, the more they stay the same."

Then Jo Ella saw Cam's eyes sharpen, and at the same moment another cheerful young male voice sounded behind her. "Hey man, I just thought I'd come over and kick your butt! What you doing here, anyway?"

"Hey, man, how about this? Hey, last I heard you was in Houston or something. You got anything to smoke?"

"Nah, wish I did. Hey, let me see your grip!"

The two boys engaged in a playful wrestling match, to the dismay of the girl, who apparently had a paper cup of Coke spilled on her textbook for her trouble. She cried, "Will you animals knock it off? Look what you did!" But the boys paid no attention.

They were all sitting too close for this kind of horseplay, and Jo Ella felt her temper began to boil as she was jostled by an elbow and had to flinch away from a flying hand. The girl got up angrily, swearing under her breath, and stalked away, and Jo Ella thought, *If they don't settle down this minute I'm going to kick somebody hard, and I know how to do it....*

At that moment one of the boys decided to flip the other over, and a pair of size-nine Nikes grazed within inches of Jo Ella's cheek and bumped Cam hard on the shoulder. Had it been any other man in this gathering of high-spirited cowboys, that would have precipitated a fistfight. Cam merely grasped the boy's ankles with a single hand and pushed him over hard. The wrestling match went on, and neither of the participants ever knew Cam had interfered.

Cam said mildly, "Why don't we go sit in the bleachers? It looks a lot more comfortable up there."

Jo Ella nodded and stood up, but as always she was a little puzzled by the nonchalantly pacifist way in which Cam handled trouble. Didn't he know that all he had to do was get to his feet and give those two punks a hard stare and they would have scurried off without a backward glance? Didn't he ever find anything worth fighting over? Didn't it ever frustrate him, knowing he was a match for any man who wanted to give it a try, to walk constantly away from threats?

Or maybe that was just it. When a man knew he could win a fight, he didn't have to prove it. Jo Ella admired that kind of quiet confidence, and she felt safe with Cam.

Jo Ella was glad they had not stayed down on the field when the concert started. Besides the fact that everyone on the field got to their feet the moment the first act stepped onstage and it would have been impossible to see anything, the people in the bleachers were much better behaved. She could relax and enjoy the concert without worrying about being trampled or hit on the head by a flying bottle or grabbed in the untrammeled excitement by the wrong man. She and Cam, like most of those around them, sang along with the lyrics and laughed and talked between numbers and generally thoroughly enjoyed themselves. The cares and the tensions of the past weeks dissolved as though they had never been, and in the space of those few hours they went back years and were young again.

Egress at the end of the concert was also much easier from the bleachers than it would have been had they been trapped in the crowds below. In only a matter of minutes, they were swept along by a tide of people onto the street.

It was an incredible sight, all those people emptying out onto the streets at one time, all heading in the same direction, like a mass exodus. It was much more impressive even than the sight of them all coming in, for then they had entered in groups of twos, threes and up to a dozen. Now it was nothing more than a mob that blocked traffic for blocks as they moved in a tight knot of hundreds, perhaps thousands, away from the arena. Cam's hand was securely on Jo Ella's back, guiding her along, protecting her from jostlers, and he talked to her cheerfully about the concert and some of the antics of the people he had seen there, and Jo Ella let herself relax and be led, confident that Cam would get them home.

"Are you hungry?" Cam asked. "Do you want to stop and get something to eat?"

For all its size, the crowd was moving pretty fast, and Jo Ella had to stretch her short legs to keep up with him. She laughed. "Are you kidding? After that hot dog feast I'll have to run two extra miles in the morning. Besides," she added, "I think there's a package of Oreos at home. Remember that?" She looked up at him, childlike eyes sparkling in the bright wash of the white streetlights. "Oreos and milk after the movies when we were kids?"

Cam laughed, urging her along with a slight pressure on her back. "Sure do. Your mom used to have them set out for us and we'd stay up for hours, sitting at the kitchen table with a plate of cookies and a jug of milk, talking or arguing or playing dominoes. Then sometimes your brothers would come down—"

"And you'd make them go back upstairs by telling scary stories. Mom never could figure out why Jimmy kept having nightmares."

"My conscience is stricken. I hope he's recovered by now."

Jo Ella had been so busy talking with Cam and trying to match his pace that she hadn't even bothered to keep up with where they were going until suddenly she looked up and nothing but black loomed before her. People were stepping into that tunnel and disappearing by droves, hundreds of them, thousands of them. She could feel them breathing and moving all around her but she couldn't see them, and suddenly time froze.

Jo Ella felt them crowding around her, she saw nothing but bodies before her, narrowing into streams and crushing into that dark tunnel. The clamor of voices became a thin buzz in her ears. Things started to close in on her, and she couldn't breathe. Her chest grew tighter and tighter until it seemed as though her ribs were crushing each other. She felt the smothering heat of a thousand bodies, blotting out her space, taking up her air, but she was cold. They pressed her from behind, they dragged her from the front, they squeezed her from either side, and Jo Ella couldn't move. A dim, desperate panic began to pound inside her—*I can't do it, I can't go in there, don't make me go in there*—and she knew if she didn't move she would be trampled, but there was no power on earth that could make her put one foot in front of the other.

She must have hesitated only a couple of seconds, for any longer than that and she literally would have been trampled by a careless and unsuspecting crowd. But Cam's arm was around her shoulders, his other arm entwined with hers. She felt the strong clasp of his hand on hers, then they were moving, somehow they were moving. Jo Ella did not remember any of it, afterward she could not have told how she ever made it through, but there was Cam's hand holding hers tightly, his strong arm sheltering her, and he was guiding her through the darkness and the hot, airless shuffle of bodies that echoed and bounced and swooped at Jo Ella like shadows of themselves, redoubling with every vibration and crowding her ears with sounds. She knew there was a scream lodged in her chest where her breath should have been, with every step she took she knew she could not take another one, everything within her rebelled; she wanted to turn and run, to break through the masses and push her way into freedom and open space. But she couldn't run, she couldn't turn, they wouldn't let her, there was no place to go, and there is no terror greater than the dark terror of the mind. Cam was holding her, Cam was guiding her, Cam was talking to her, but she only heard the low soothing murmur of his voice, none of the words. She only felt the clasp of his hand on hers, and it was a lifeline. And somehow he got her through.

Outside the tunnel the crowd began to disperse in various directions toward separate parking lots, and Cam casually led Jo Ella to the grass lining the sidewalk, letting the thinning crowd pass them by at a more rapid pace. "Umm, smell that night air," he said. "Take a deep breath, Jocy. Doesn't it taste good?"

His voice filtered down to her as she stood in a locked paralysis of residual terror, her feet moving numbly with his out of habit, not will. And out of habit she obeyed his gentle suggestion, and the rush of cold air to her burning lungs jarred her back from the verge of unconsciousness. She started shaking then, trying hard to control the shuddering gasps for air, knowing she was in danger of hyperventilation if she did not. She felt the dampness of her sweater, which only increased her shivering, but the cold air was so good she drank it in like a drowning man; she couldn't get enough. And Cam still held her, guiding her along at an easy, casual pace, keeping her walking to regulate the pace of her breathing. "Getting chilly out, isn't it?" he commented when Jo Ella had managed to bring her breathing under control enough to hear him. She was still shivering. He stopped, and very gently pried her fingers off his hand so he could shrug out of his jacket. Jo Ella saw the bright red crescents her fingernails had left on his smooth skin, but the trauma had been too great this time for her to be embarrassed. She merely looked up at him in mute gratitude and apology, but Cam only smiled and draped the heavy jacket over her shoulders.

Cam needed no apology, no explanation. He simply understood, as he always had, and he knew what she needed even before she did. Cam had known how to get her through the tunnel. He had known how to keep her from succumbing to hysteria afterward. He understood this horrible frailty that Jo Ella had never been able to confess to anyone, and he had been there for her. And Jo Ella loved him, at that moment, more than she ever had in her entire life.

She loved him, but it was more than that. The understanding draped over her like something soft and shimmering and warm, and with it came a whole new vista of emotions and thoughts and sensations. With it came the awesome realization of what had been happening to her, growing slowly within her, for perhaps all of her life. She loved him with the wild and soaring passion that his touch could incite, with the euphoria only being in his presence could generate, with the passion that made her yearn for intimacy. It was the live wire of sexuality, the temporary chemical madness of attraction. That she had always known. But it was also something quiet and steady and sure, a still stream running deep, something intangible that bound her to him no matter how many years or miles separated them. It was the handclasp of a friend in a dark and lonely place. She needed him. She needed him with the quick, hot urgency of desire and with the strong, silent yearning of emptiness. He was her ballast in a storm-tossed world, he was the other side of the coin, he was what made her complete.

But with new understanding came new responsibility, and it was under the weight of this realization that Jo Ella remained dazedly silent on the way back to the car and for most of the trip home. Cam was everything that was real and sure and important to her, but what could Jo Ella be for him? He gave her security and quiet common sense, a calm refuge from life's battering currents, something to hold on to when her world was sifting down like ashes around her feet. When she fell, he was always there to catch her. And she gave him... what? She flitted in and out of his life at whim, upsetting his carefully balanced routine, making demands and spreading discontent, inviting promises but unwilling to give any of her own. And then leaving him, until the next time. He wanted peace and she gave him uproar. He valued simplicity and she brought complications. Into his low-key, conservative life-style she brought scandal and notoriety, and she had no right to do that to him.

It had taken her twenty-seven years to realize that she was slowly destroying the only man she had ever loved.

"You're looking better," Cam said, and Jo Ella brought her thoughts slowly spiraling back to the present. The lights of Dallas flickered and shadowed his face, that strong, competent face that was completely in control whether it be negotiating the dangers of downtown traffic or the dark tunnels of someone else's mind.

Jo Ella's smile was a little wan but very grateful. That was the first time he had mentioned the episode directly, or even overtly acknowledged it. With typical insight he had known that anything he could have said previously would only have made Jo Ella think about her fear and make matters worse, so he had treated it casually. But now that she had recovered he knew she needed to talk about it, and he was offering her the opportunity. He always knew just what to do.

"I don't know what causes it," Jo Ella said, and that simple statement, bringing it out into the open and recognizing that the problem existed, was all she needed to say. Just knowing she could talk about it made her feel better. "I've tried to figure it out, you know, but I can't find any reason. No traumatic experiences in childhood, no repressed resentments or anxieties..." She shook her head helplessly. "Good old Dr. Freud seems to be at a complete loss on this one. It just happens."

Cam lifted one shoulder negligently. "Who knows what makes the mind tick? I guess everyone has at least one bad phobia. For me, it's heights."

Jo Ella looked at him, amazed. "Really?"

He flashed her a brief, easy grin. "You never knew that? Anything higher than a stepladder and I break out in a cold sweat."

Jo Ella found that hard to digest. She had never thought of Cam as anything but invincible. That he should have fears and weaknesses just as irrational as her own was nothing short of incredible. "But," she protested, "you're not afraid of flying. You'll go up in an airplane."

He laughed. "An airplane, sure—preferably a seven-forty-seven with no windows. But you'd have to knock me out first, and then hog-tie me, to get me on one of those damn helicopters. If I can look down and see anything but my own feet I turn into a block of ice. Total brain fade." And he glanced at her, his grin easy and companionable. "Now that you know my weakness, are you going to exploit it?"

"Do I do that, Cam?" she asked softly, looking at him. "Do I exploit you?"

Brief bewilderment flickered in his eyes at the odd question, but it was quickly replaced with acceptance, if not understanding, of the reason for it. He smiled and captured her fingers lightly, brushing them across his lips with casual affection. "Hardly ever," he assured her.

It was the only truthful answer he could have given her, Jo Ella knew. But it wasn't good enough.

"So how about those cookies?" Cam invited when they were inside the apartment, lamps glowing warmly, the hands of the clock inching toward midnight.

Jo Ella hesitated for only a moment. She thought about that, Cam and she across the kitchen table late at night with cookies and milk, easing into a less complicated time by reliving the scenes of their past.... She smiled. "I don't think so, Cam. I'm kind of tired. I think I'll just go to bed." No, past and present had crossed and linked too much tonight as it was, and things were not quite so simple anymore. Tonight she needed time alone to try to sort it all out.

Cam looked momentarily surprised, then slightly confused, as though he had only this moment glimpsed something troubling about Jo Ella. She thought he would question her, for directness was usually Cam's way when he thought she was hiding something, but instead he only smiled. "Sure thing. It's been a long night."

She returned his smile and started toward the bedroom. But midway there she stopped. While nothing else was clear, this one thing remained. It was the very least she owed him. "Cam," she said, turning. He paused on his way to the television set to look at her. "Thanks for tonight and"—she took a breath, her voice softening—"I just wanted you to know that... I've always loved you."

And she turned quickly and went into the bedroom, not wanting to see whatever emotion was in his eyes. She did not want to cause him more discomfort, or more obligation. That one thing from her was given freely.

She picked out her nightclothes absently, folded her jeans and sweater neatly on a chair and slipped her nightgown over her head. She gave her hair a few perfunctory strokes with the hairbrush, but her movements were cottony and slow, as though she were walking in a daze. And she was not thinking anything clearly, she was only feeling. What she was feeling was a single syllable, a single entity, and it seemed to permeate her whole being, heart, mind and soul: *Cam.*

She was just folding back the covers on Cam's bed when there was a soft knock at the door. Her heart caught, and she straightened up slowly. It was as though the very power of her yearning had drawn him to her. It was a moment before she could answer, "Come in."

Cam opened the door. His stance was casual and his expression relaxed, but Jo Ella could sense—or perhaps she only imagined—something different about him, an underlying tension or an uncertainty, or perhaps even an expectation.

Jo Ella's princess-style nightgown was flesh-colored cotton, full-sleeved and low-necked. She did not mistake the way his eyes flickered over her figure, registering recognition and the briefest stab of desire, and Jo Ella was suddenly, irrationally shy. She did not want to draw attention to the fact by making a mad scramble for her robe, so she merely sat on the edge of the bed, tucking one leg beneath her in what seemed to her a less revealing pose. But when Cam smiled at her, there was nothing in his eyes to indicate this was to be anything more than a casual visit—which, of course, was exactly what it was.

"Short notice, I know," he said, "but I was just wondering—would you like to go for a drive in the country in the morning?"

Something quivered within Jo Ella that felt insanely like disappointment, but she dismissed it quickly. "Sure," she responded easily. "Where to?"

"Surprise," he answered with an enigmatic wink. "But we'll have to leave early. Six o'clock?"

She groaned dramatically and buried her face briefly in the pillow. "It had better be good," she warned him, sitting up again.

"Oh, I think it is," he answered, and then something gentled in his face, lightened in his eyes, and it held Jo Ella hypnotized. It was as though she could feel what he was feeling at that moment, think what he was thinking, and the moment between them shifted and changed like a lens going from soft-focus to closeup, binding them together for a single frame in time. Anticipation and certainty, hope and fear, need and caution, all were reflected in his eyes and crept slowly into Jo Ella's soul.

"That's a very pretty nightgown," he said softly, and he began to move toward her.

The telephone rang, and the moment, like so many others between them, was gone. Cam continued to move toward the telephone on the night table as though that had been his original intention all along, and there was nothing in his voice but a casual greeting as he answered it.

Jo Ella carefully unclenched her tight fists as he stood there, half turned from her, within inches but too far away to touch. She tried not to think what might have happened had the moment been allowed to spin itself out to its natural conclusion, for it hurt too much to look into the future. She would have to learn to accept things for what they were.

Cam was saying, "Well, that was quick, wasn't it?" and he was grinning. Jo Ella felt a brief shaft of disappointment that it wasn't a wrong number. If it had been only a short interruption, there might have been a chance.... But she refused to think about that.

"Well, congratulations, old man," Cam said, and Jo Ella's attention sharpened. It was Burt. "How's Mary... That's great. Just great." Another pause while Burt presumably gave him all those details that no one but the father ever remembers, and Cam said, "Well, you tell her we'll be by to see her in the next couple of days. You take care now. And congratulations again."

Cam replaced the receiver and turned to her. Was that a hint of regret behind his smile—regret for the lost moment, disappointment for what might have been? Or perhaps he was grateful that the real world had intruded on a fantasy, saving him from a momentary lapse of judgment. But whatever it was was transitory, and there was nothing but pleasure and pride in his renewed unclehood as he told her, grinning, "It's a girl."

Chapter Nine

Jo Ella straightened up, tilted her sunglasses and looked curiously out the window. "Good heavens," she said, "I've never seen so many trees." And then, blinking the daze of sleep from her eyes, "Why, they're pecan trees, aren't they? And it's harvesttime!"

"Yep," agreed Cam, his hand negligently guiding the pickup truck over the rutted dirt road. "Bet you didn't know this part of Texas is the biggest producer of pecans in the world."

"Sure I did," Jo Ella scoffed, but in actuality it amazed her. So much of the land surrounding Dallas was arid and barren, it was something of a shock to come upon an orchard of these proportions in the middle of nowhere—nothing but rows and rows of trees as far as the eye could see. Work crews and mechanized pickers moved industriously through the rows even on this Sunday morning, and Cam received smiles and waves as he tapped his horn and lifted his hand as they passed.

Jo Ella had slept for most of the two-and-a-half-hour trip, and Cam had let her. The morning sun was brightening away the chill of the day now, and the fresh air streaming through Cam's lowered window brought her wide awake. He hadn't once let slip a single hint about where they were going, though Jo Ella assumed it would be an all-day excursion when he loaded a cooler into the back of the truck. When he had turned off the highway, onto an unmarked road and finally to this dirt road that seemed to go nowhere but deeper and deeper into the pecan grove, Jo Ella was more confused than ever. "Is this where we're going, then?" she queried at last. "To a pecan orchard?"

Cam chuckled. "Almost."

Cam was in an extraordinarily good mood today. He had been singing tunes from last night's concert when he woke Jo Ella at five-thirty, and whistling as he loaded the truck in the cold morning twilight. His fingers kept rhythm on the steering wheel with the low volume of the radio, and the sun sparkled in his eyes. It was as though he had left a visible burden of cares and worries behind the locked apartment door, and Jo Ella could not remember when she had seen him so relaxed.

"If I didn't know for a fact," she commented, "that you didn't pack your fishing poles, I'd swear there was a stocked lake up ahead."

He glanced at her with a twinkle. "What makes you say that?"

"Because the last time—no, the only time," she corrected, "I saw you this happy was when you were on your way for a weekend fishing expedition."

He laughed, and his fingers came out to capture hers, swinging them lightly, a few inches above the seat, for a moment, before releasing them. "Why shouldn't I be happy?" he challenged. "My brother just brought into the world a healthy baby girl—"

"With a little help," Jo Ella interjected dryly.

Cam cheerfully ignored her. "It's a beautiful day and I'm with a beautiful woman...." He glanced at her again, and the dancing warmth in his eyes tingled through her with a swift rush of pleasure. "No rain forecast for the next week, and the harvest is going to be the best ever."

Jo Ella's eyes widened abruptly with understanding. "Cam," she said in delighted amazement, "this pecan field—you mean it's *yours*?"

Cam brought the truck to a jolting halt, slammed it in gear and opened the door, grabbing her hand. "Come on," he said, and his eyes were brilliant and dazzling as he tugged her across the seat toward him. "I want to show you something."

Jo Ella tumbled out of the truck and saw they were standing in the middle of a clearing at the end of the orchard. Earth movers had been in recently to level the ground, and the sandy loam was flanked on one side by neatly stacked scrub brush and saplings. Small, red-flagged stakes marked a rectangular area in the center of the clearing, and at the far end stood a small utility building. And behind it, above it, around it as far as the eye could see was nothing but open space.

"Why," Jo Ella said softly, "it looks like—"

"The beginnings of my house," Cam explained, and he draped his arm over her shoulders, walking across the scrubby, rock-strewn ground toward the flagged stakes. "I went into partnership with this guy on the pecan grove a few years ago," he went on, "and it's turned out pretty well—well enough that I was able to buy this property here. And after this harvest I'll be able to buy my partner out." There was quiet pride in his voice even as he gave a low chuckle. "This time next year I'll be a full-fledged independent pecan farmer. How do you like the sound of that?"

Jo Ella was speechless with wonder and admiration, but she could not say she was overwhelmed with surprise. Cameron, the builder—what else? She had often wondered over the years why he kept himself in a small apartment when she knew his biggest ambition was to own a home, why he lived such a limited life-style when she knew the air-charter service was thriving and he earned more in a month than she did in a year.... She gave him a sly, delighted look. "And here I was thinking you were burying your money in Mason jars in the back yard all these years. I should have known better!"

He grinned at her. "You sure should have. Wipe your feet, we're going into the living room."

Jo Ella made a great show of dusting off her shoes on the imaginary welcome mat while Cam opened an imaginary door with a flourish and gestured her inside. "You are looking," he informed her, "at a full-wall stone fireplace à la Ponderosa. To your left is a spiral staircase that leads to a study and two bedrooms upstairs. Turn around—you'll love the view from the picture window."

Jo Ella turned and she caught her breath slowly. She had not realized before that they had been traveling up a small incline, and the view overlooked a vista of dusky purple desert, dull-green trees and cobalt sky, all in layers like a rich dessert. The openness and space that swam endlessly before her was dizzying, intoxicating, heartstoppingly beautiful. Cam stood beside her, his arm around her shoulders, his contentment seeping into her with each shared breath, and they absorbed the beauty of the open sky and rich earth, the promise of his dream. Jo Ella turned to him, her eyes flowing. "I love it, Cam," she said softly.

He wrapped his arms around her, drawing her gently close, and the depth of joy in his eyes was peaceful and eternal, it encompassed the air and the earth and the woman in his arms, it fell over Jo Ella like the warmth of the climbing sun. His lips were soft upon hers, tasting her tenderly and with leisure, drawing out the moment into an interlocking network of sensation and emotion not to be rushed, only to be savored. Jo Ella knew she was clinging to him, melting into him, but her body seemed to be dispersing, losing contact with the earth beneath her feet, dissolving into a million tiny particles that transported her above this place and outside this moment. She was free of mortal bonds, unfettered by clumsy flesh, she was only consciousness, and all of her was concentrated into nothing more than the sensation of Cam's lips upon hers. Lightly, softly, endlessly, he created eternity from nothing more than a kiss. She felt the soft sucking motion that drew her lower lip into his mouth, she tasted the warm, sweet sweep of his tongue and the tingle of his breath filling her mouth. He took her as a man would an expensive gourmet feast, with deliberation and delicacy and expert attention to the finest sensual detail. He held her as though he had every intention of drawing her inside him inch by inch and cell by cell, as though he could open up her pores and let her very essence flow into him by osmosis, as though this kiss could go on forever. And he was not wrong.

It took Jo Ella a long time to realize he was no longer kissing her, and a longer time still for the fragmented parts of her consciousness to coalesce in the real world again. She felt the wind in her hair, the sun on her shoulders. She felt the pulsing of her heart and the radiance of her skin, and she could still taste him in every part of her. Cam's hands were cupping her face, his eyes were deep and quiet and tender. She could see a vein on his forehead that was faintly enlarged as though from exertion, she could feel the restraint in the muscles of his arms and the slow, deliberate rhythm of his breath. There was a low-burning flame of hunger in his eyes that he did not bother to disguise, but above it all there was peace on his face, simple contentment, the timeless lack of urgency of one who weighs his decisions carefully and sees the future clearly.

He dropped his hands from Jo Ella's face, and his smile was slow and sure and tender as he slipped one arm around her waist. "Let me show you the rest of the house," he said.

They walked arm in arm through imaginary rooms, Cam sketching walls and floor out of thin air and Jo Ella contributing a generous number of windows. Cam laid the floors and Jo Ella enlarged the closets by half, and they negligently tossed in a swimming pool and a Jacuzzi for good measure. Jo Ella laughed out loud for no other reason than that she was happy.

They continued to walk, hands loosely linked, heads tossed back to the wind, across the stubbly ground, over small hills and endless flat terrain, past a clean, narrow creek with a natural pool, and Jo Ella asked, "How much property do you own, anyway?"

"Besides the orchard? Twenty-seven acres," he answered. "I'd like to have horses, eventually. Cross-fence this section and that..." He was standing on the edge of an incline, his arm lifted to point out the acres to her, but Jo Ella was not watching the terrain. She was watching Cam, and the way the breeze molded his shirt to his body and lifted his hair away from his strong profile. Jo Ella knew she would remember the way he looked at that moment forever—strong and solid against the wind, his hand outstretched over the vastness below him, man and sky and earth in harmony. It was raw, it was vibrant, it was free—and it stirred something deep within Jo Ella's soul.

The sun was getting high in the sky by the time they had circled around and the pickup was in view again, but neither of them felt the strain of the walk. For Jo Ella it was as though her feet had not once touched the ground. Being with Cam in this place, feeling his hand closing on hers, sharing his dreams and building his future had transported her into a world she had never dared imagine before. It was a world where she belonged.

It was noon when Cam unpacked the cooler and they spread a blanket on the ground in the sun, sharing a picnic feast of beer and sandwiches of thick-sliced ham and cheese. "I spend most of my weekends out here," Cam told her. He was sitting with one knee propped up and his arm resting on it, a beer bottle held negligently in his dangling hand. His eyes were squinted toward the sun, and when he glanced at her in quick recollection the dancing sun-sparks obscured any apology that might have been there. "Or at least I did," he amended, "until—"

"Until I moved in," she finished for him, without reproach. She passed him another sandwich, then asked him, purely out of curiousity, "Why did you never tell me about this place?"

He shrugged, pushing back the wrappings on the sandwich with one hand. "I don't know. You had so much on your mind, and I didn't think you'd be around long enough to..." But he trailed off there, not finishing, and after a moment he turned his attention to the sandwich.

Jo Ella tried not to be hurt. He was right. She had never stayed long enough to make any difference in his life, and anything he might share with her could only be in passing. How much of the important things had she missed about Cam over the years because she simply was never around long enough to get involved? It was a haunting, empty feeling, and the hunger she felt now had nothing to do with food. If only there were some way to make up for lost time, to cram into this one day all the things about him she had missed before....

"So," she said, refusing to let anything, whether it be regrets from the past or clouds over the future, blur the perfection of this day. "When are you planning to move in?"

"By spring, I hope." He finished off his sandwich

and wadded up the paper. "I'm trying to get the house framed in before bad weather, and I should have clear title to the orchard by January. From there"—he grinned, draining the last of his beer—"it's onward and upward."

Jo Ella lifted her eyebrows appreciatively. "What does Burt think about this?"

"He's my brother," Cam answered simply. "He approves."

"No regrets about losing his top mechanic and only partner?"

Cam laughed and opened two more beers, handing one to her as he explained the complicated business dealings that would allow him to continue to own part of the company while giving Burt full managerial control. Jo Ella tried to pay attention, but the beer and the sunshine and the sheer pleasure of being with him were combining into mellowness, and she lay down on the blanket, one arm folded to support her cheek, and smiled at him. "Funny," she mused. "I never knew you were so smart about business before. I mean, I guess I knew it, I just never thought about it. I've learned a lot about you the last couple of days, and I thought I knew everything."

Cam looked down at her. The sun drew a pinkish translucence from her skin, and her eyes seemed to absorb its rays until they were like glowing velvet. Her smile was sleepy and content, and her hair so bathed with light that he thought if he touched it it would burn his hand. Jo Ella belonged here, in all this space and sunshine, the sky surrounding her, the earth below her. Cam wanted to remember her like this always.

He smiled at her indulgently. "Like what?"

"Oh, like..." She shifted her cheek more comfortably on her arm so that she could look at him. "You're afraid of heights, your secret ambition is to be a pecan farmer, you're a positive genius at matters of finance and business...."

He chuckled. "I wouldn't go so far as that," he said, but his eyes were sparkling, and when he looked at her Jo Ella had the impression he had not really heard anything she had said. He continued to look at her, and then suddenly, subtly, the sparkle in his eyes changed, became softer and more introspective, as though he was seeing something not visible to the naked eye. Even the muscles of his face changed, becoming more malleable yet in some way harder, as though he had just discovered something disturbing in her face or in the pose of her body. Jo Ella felt her own muscles responding to the change within him, a whisper of tension passing through her that felt more like a tingle of anticipation; she could not prevent the hesitant half-question in her eyes. And then Cam looked away.

"I've learned a few things about you, too," he said quietly.

Jo Ella was not certain she wanted to hear. She sat up slowly, and her voice, which she had meant to be so casual was almost a whisper. "Like what?"

Cam looked for a moment at the bottle of beer he held loosely by the neck between his knees. Then he moved his eyes briefly to hers, and away again to examine the horizon. "What you said last night," he answered. "You've never said that to me before."

Jo Ella felt a peculiar thump in her chest that was

only her heart trying to keep up with her racing emotions. Hadn't she? Had she never told Cam before that she loved him? No, of course not. Jo Ella, light of foot and free of care, would have just assumed he knew.

"Someone once said," Cam went on in an even, quietly reflective tone, "that the difference between a friend and a lover is that when a friend says 'I love you' you don't have to ask what he means."

Jo Ella drew in her breath, her hand half reaching for him, but he looked at her, and the quiet complacency in his eyes stopped her. "No," he said, and his lips softened in what might have been the beginning of a smile. "That wasn't a request. I think things are a little too overdefined in my life as it is. Maybe I need less structure and more open spaces." And he looked away again.

"What do you want it to mean, Cam?" Jo Ella asked softly.

He was silent for a moment, and then he said simply, without looking back at her, "I'm not sure."

Jo Ella wanted to touch him, to take his face in her hands and make him look at her, to force him to reveal in his eyes what he would not with his words. She wanted him to know, she wanted him to tell her what he wanted and in return she wanted to give it to him. But she wouldn't touch him. She wouldn't force herself on him. She drew her knees up and wrapped her arms around them, resting her cheek on her crossed arms. She stayed silent as long as she could, but the tension was building inside her like a vise slowly squeezing her heart; her emotions and her needs were swelling to break the confines of their cage. And Cam was silent, lost in his own meditation. When she did not think she could bear it any longer, she said, softly, "What are you thinking?"

Again she saw that slow, lazy smile begin to trace its curve along his lips. He was smiling to himself and at himself, and she wanted desperately for him to share the private source of that smile with her. "Right this minute?" he queried, still not looking at her.

She nodded. "Uh-huh. Right this minute."

She saw the brief lowering of his lashes, the gentle dimpling of his cheek. "I was thinking," he confessed, "how much fun we used to have before..." She knew he intended to say something else, but he finished simply. "Before." And then he went on unexpectedly, in the same casual, reflective tone. "I was thinking how good you taste and wondering whether you still put perfume behind your knees like you used to; I was thinking that I want to taste every inch of you. I was thinking how badly I want to make love to you and trying to remember all the reasons I shouldn't, and you know what?" He turned to her, his eyes alight with a deep and subtle inner glow, his voice husky. "I couldn't think of a single one."

He placed his hand upon her upraised knees, and before Jo Ella could take a breath he had lowered them to the ground with a gentle pressure. His face swam before her, very close. "Do you mind?" he whispered, and his rough hand caressed her cheek.

Jo Ella thought she shook her head, but her mute response was lost in the next moment by the sudden heady surge of wonder and dizziness generated by the mesmerizing power of his fingertips.

It was Cam's intention to be very gentle with her, to draw out every nuance of pleasure from the experience for himself and for her. In lovemaking, as in every other part of his life, Cam was always tender and controlled. And he began that way. His fingers lightly traced each part of her he adored before the brush of his tongue completed the pattern—the delicately veiled orbs of her eyes and the soft fringe of lashes, the small sweeping angle of her nose, the curve of her ear, the softness of parted lips. He could feel her shallow breath mingling with his, see the sun-flush of color tingeing her skin. He could feel small, warm hands against his throat. His weight lightly shadowed her, protecting her, and his hair brushed her face as he bent his head to follow with his tongue the small firm ridges of her throat to its soft base; he felt her gasp as he lingered his attention there. His hands slipped beneath her sweater, dragging it upward and over her head, and then she was his, exposed to the sun and the sky and the worshipful pleasure of his gaze.

Jo Ella had thought it would be easy to slip with him back into a relationship that was their natural right. She thought it would be sweet and simple and fairy-tale soft, as she had remembered it, as it had always been. But from the moment she saw the dark light of intention in his eyes, from the moment she felt the first touch of his lips upon her skin, she was consumed by a high-burning fever, shattered by the rush of a thundering pulse and shaky limbs and drowning in a tangle of emotions and sensations that she hardly recognized at all. She wanted it to be beautiful, she wanted to remember every detail and experience every sensation to its fullest, most exquisite point. She tried to remember to breathe, she tried to still her restless hands, which wanted to clutch and roam and urge; she tried to relax the urgency and slow the galloping, erratic demands of her pounding heart. But she felt Cam's hands tracing the outline of her ribs; she felt the warmth of his mouth covering her breasts, and a red-black need twisted in her abdomen, robbed her of breath, building and spreading and consuming her reason, blotting out everything but Cam and her desperation for him. Her hands fumbled beneath his shirt, greedily clutching at bare skin and tracing smooth contours, pressing the shape of his buttocks beneath the heavy denim, then clumsily, eagerly finding the strong cords of the back of his neck, tracing them, cupping them, pushing him down to her.

She felt the exploding tension within him, his quick catch of breath, the heat that fanned through him and redoubled her own. She felt the urgency of his hands pressing into her waist and his mouth drawing on her breasts, spurring her upward to new heights of gasping pleasure, and she knew something was happening to them, and between them, that had never been before. His touch was blinding her, as hers was him, pulling them deeper and faster into unexplored regions, for when they thought they knew all there was to know about each other the urgency of the promise was that there was yet more to be discovered. Cam's fingers pulled at the catch of her jeans, and the zipper opened with a soft, grating sound. His hand pressed and kneaded the flesh of her lower abdomen and his tongue tasted the skin above, circling and probing her navel, making her shiver and gasp for breath. He dragged her jeans down over her hips, exposing more of her to his taste and his touch; then he sat up and stripped them off her ankles urgently, tossing them aside to be joined only seconds later by his own.

Cam was by nature a tender lover. He was actually aware of his own strength and size and of Jo Ella's fragility, both emotional and physical. In this, as in all other areas of his life, his passions were always tempered by care; he knew how easily he could hurt another without meaning to or even trying. He meant to love Jo Ella as he had always loved her—carefully, gently, with intensity but with control. But suddenly she was pressing against him and moving against him, his senses were filled wih the taste and scent of her, and control slipped away; deeper needs and unsuspected passions shook him, blinded him, stripped away all caution and filled him with mindless needs and basic instincts that knew no course except their own satisfaction. He heard her cry out when he thrust inside her, and something deep within his fast-fading consciousness registered alarm, but then she was rising to meet him, wrapping her legs and her arms around him, taking as greedily from him as he was from her. Then all reason was blotted out, he was drowning within her; he drove his hands deep into her hair and pulled her head back to receive his kiss, and he thought he heard his own voice growl into her mouth, "Mine...only mine..."

Mine, Jo Ella echoed in a rush of joy that was fast spiraling to blot out the sun. *You're mine....* And that was the last clear thought she had as his mouth swallowed hers, his body drove hers, and his demand met and fired her own, taking her above and beyond all that was real, all that was coherent, taking her outside herself and into him and the need for him. Borders blurred and disappeared, boundaries were transcended as they blended into one another and all that was around them, and they surged higher and higher until the sky itself seemed to open up and draw them in.

As with the most intense experiences of one's life, Jo Ella was to find that afterward, as much as she wanted to and as hard as she tried, she could not remember the details of that endless time she was locked in Cam's arms and captured in his need. She remembered it was primal and violent, shattering and stunning them both, it was uncontrolled and all-powerful. It transcended anything either of them had ever known before. It seemed, for a time, as if their very souls touched and in the joining revealed things about themselves and each other neither had ever guessed before. It did not fade gently into fulfillment; it exploded between them, and the white-hot impact paled the sun in comparison, forging them together for all time.

Fragments of her consciousness floated high above the earth in an airborne dance with his, drifting, weightless, touching, joining, settling on gossamer wings slowly back into sun-drenched, perspiration-cooled bodies. She heard the thin flow of his breathing, felt the weight of his hand across her thigh. Sunlight pulsed in her eyes to the rhythm of her heart, a breeze touched her cheek. Cam was all around her, the feel and the taste and the scent of him. He still filled every pore, every cell; he was all of her.

Cam could not move, he could not think; he could not accept what had just happened between them. He had never behaved like that with any woman . . . he had never felt like that with any woman. He could feel her muscles still quivering beneath his hand. Had he hurt her? What had happened to him? His actions had been those of a man possessed—or one who wishes to possess. He had never felt like that before.

Had he really muttered those demanding, possessive words to her? Had he really held this fragile bird in his hands with enough strength to crush? Yes, it had been he. He had done those things, those harsh and wild and uncivilized things because at that moment he had wanted to possess her, he had wanted to brand her as his own, he had wanted to hold her and never let her go. . . .

Cam could feel the pulse in his abdomen jerking under his splayed hand, his breath grating in his ears. Until that moment he had been detached from his own body, free of conscience and consciousness, and now he could not believe what had happened to him—to them. Had it been only a matter of days ago that he had so callously accused Jo Ella of bartering sex? But in the end who had used whom to get what he wanted? He had sworn he would never do that. Sex was his only hold on her, it was the one way he could be sure of keeping her to himself for just a while longer. It was symbolic in its domination and bonding; it was the strongest tie a man could have with a woman. He had known that, and he had used it. He had wanted to possess her, and he had.

Cam sat up, weak with a sudden flood of shame and

remorse; he reached for his jeans. "It's getting cold out here," he said. His voice was a little husky. "Better get dressed."

Her fingers, feather-light, trailed along his bare arm. He shivered. "I don't think I can," she murmured. He could hear the sleepy smile in her voice, and a sudden wave of love and need so powerful it shook him swept over him; he turned to look at her.

The agonized regret and apology on his face faded slowly and softened at the sight of her; it was gone completely before she opened her eyes. She was so lovely, so tiny, and all he wanted to do was protect her, to shelter her and love her, to make her feel warm and secure and to bring her happiness wherever he could. He just wanted to love her.

He smiled when she opened her eyes; he gently brushed her hair away from her forehead. "I'm sorry I was so rough," he said. His voice was a little hoarse and not quite even. Anxiety crept back into his eyes as he scanned her body, looking for marks on her skin or pain in her face. She saw his fear, and her teasing smile coaxed his worry away. She sat up, cupping his shoulders with her hands, pressing her lips to his back. "You're forgiven," she said. "Providing..."

He let her touch relax him, her smile soothe away his anxiety. He knew it was wrong. He knew it couldn't last. The kind of imprisonment he was trying to force on her was no way to express the love he felt for her, and soon he would begin to see it in her eyes, the resentment, the restlessness, the trapped feeling. But right now all he saw in her eyes was contentment, and right now all he wanted to do was to let it last as long as it could, to take the moment for all it was worth. That was all he had ever been able to do with Jo Ella.

He turned, slipping his arms around her waist and drawing her next to him. He wished he could hold her like this, naked in the sunshine, forever. But his smile was a little uncertain as he inquired, "Providing what?"

She traced the shape of his hairline with her fingertip, felt the scar just above his temple. She looked at him seriously. "Providing," she told him, "you take me home to your own bed and start all over again."

His grin was slow and easy and delightful. "It gets better," he promised.

"It couldn't," she returned soberly, and he laughed. She wrapped her arms around his neck; she kissed him. And she whispered quietly, drawing her mouth away from his just slightly, "I do love you, Cam. I really do."

Cam buried his face in her neck and tightened his arms around her once, fiercely, then he gradually made himself loosen the embrace until he was barely holding her, barely touching her. He could not return the words to her. His own emotions were too powerful, too confusing, and he needed time to get them under control. He would not offer her love with chains, and that, at the moment, was all he had.

Chapter Ten

The next two weeks were so blissful, so perfect, that Jo Ella should have known they couldn't last. She and Cam were in a world of their own, wrapped in passion-hazed discovery-filled nights that lingered deliriously throughout their days, dazzling them with euphoria and wonder and blinding them to anything outside themselves and their perfect contentment. Nothing could go wrong. Everything clicked. Jo Ella's mother did not call to depress her, Burt and Mary settled in easily with the new baby, the foundation was poured on Cam's house without a hitch. But if everything had gone wrong; if rains had ruined the harvest and flooded the building site, if Jo Ella's mother had decided to move in with them, if all the helicopters were grounded at a cost of thousands of dollars a day, neither Cam nor Jo Ella would have cared or, in all likelihood, noticed. That was the magic of being in love.

And because everything was so supernaturally perfect, Jo Ella was not surprised when Mrs. Bernell called with an interview that sounded too good to be true, nor was she surprised to find herself sailing through the interview and actually receiving a job offer. Jo Ella was walking on air when she came home that afternoon, singing softly to herself as she tossed her coat on a chair and went into the kitchen to put the coffee on. Cam would not be home for a couple of hours yet, and . . .

She gasped out loud in surprise and then delight as a strong hand covered her eyes from behind and warm lips pressed against the back of her neck. "Cam!" she exclaimed, wiggling out of his half-embrace to wind her arms around his neck and greet him properly. Her eyes were dancing with excitement and pleasure, and her color was high as she tilted her face up to look at him. "What are you doing home so early?"

"I'm a boss," he returned, playfully landing a kiss on her nose. "We're allowed to do that. I just thought," he explained, "I'd surprise my favorite lady with flowers"—from behind his back he whipped out a bouquet of sweetheart roses, which Jo Ella accepted with a cry of delight—"and champagne." He took a glass of bubbling golden liquid from the counter and presented it to her with a flourish. "And my own expertise with a frozen dinner." He grinned. "Any objections?"

Jo Ella laughed, balancing her attention between the fragrance of the roses and the champagne glass and his lips, which were nibbling at her neck. The roses were sacrificed between their bodies as she turned her mouth to his for a kiss, but she saved most of the champagne by holding it in the hand that lifted to encircle his neck.

"Mmm," Cam murmured, lifting his face at last. His

eyes were half closed and his fingers curved around her hips, cradling her into his pelvis. "Roses every day—champagne twice a week."

Jo Ella laughed, a bubbling sound that sprang upward from the tips of her toes and was generated by sheer happiness. "And," she announced, stepping away from him to find a vase for the slightly crushed roses, "we actually have something to celebrate!" She took a sip of her champagne and lifted the glass to him, her eyes sparkling. "I got a job!" Jo Ella was too excited to notice the concern of alarm that flickered across Cam's eyes, and she did not give him a chance to say anything before she finished, "With a travel agency, right here in town!"

Then there was nothing but relief in Cam's eyes, her shared happiness, and he picked up his own champagne glass, touching it to hers. "Now that," he declared with enthusiasm, "I can drink to. I couldn't have picked a better job for you myself. Tell me all the details."

"Well, the position doesn't come open until next month," she went on, and took another sip of her champagne. "Expensive stuff," she interrupted herself with an an appreciative lift of the brow. "Delicious." And so were the tantalizing motions he was making with his fingers around the waistband of her skirt.

"Only the best for a special occasion like this," he insisted, and his fingers toyed with her zipper.

Jo Ella laughed, reminding herself about the vase for the roses, and she put down her champagne glass as she went to get it. "You didn't even know it was a special occasion!" she accused.

"Every day with you is a special occasion," he insisted gallantly, and leaning negligently against the counter, he traced the pattern of her ribs as she lifted her arms to the cabinet for the vase.

Jo Ella started to giggle and twist away, and the ringing of the telephone interrupted their play. Jo Ella, who was closest, answered it.

It was Cam's mother. "Jo Ella," she fretted, "I've been trying to reach you all day."

"I'm sorry, Mrs. Scott." Jo Ella straightened up and pushed Cam's roving hand away, just as though the esteemed lady could see through the telephone and into their kitchen. "I had an interview and I got a—"

"The most terrible thing has happened, and I just don't know what to do," Avis interrupted her, sounding distraught. Jo Ella's attention quickened, and she moved her neck away from Cam's distracting lips, frowning a little with concern. "You remember I told you about Marshall?"

"That was Marianne's ex-husband, wasn't it?" Jo Ella was getting pretty good at sorting out the complicated lives of Avis Scott's neighbors. She wondered what could have possibly happened to get Cam's mother upset. "The last I heard he was threatening to get custody of their son."

"Oh, it's terrible, just terrible," Avis moaned. Jo Ella heard her sniffle. "He came by today when he thought Marianne wasn't there and he told the babysitter to go home—he was going to kidnap that child! He was going to take him right out of his bed and he almost did it, too, but Marianne came home early and oh, there was the most awful fight! The poor child started screaming and ran under the bed and Marshall was yelling the most awful things and making terrible threats and Marianne was hysterical—well, you can just imagine!" Cam started playing with the clasp of Jo Ella's bra, but she shrugged away, intent upon the unfolding drama. "And I guess he didn't know that she's carried a gun in her purse ever since she started working nights and there have been so many attacks on the streets because—"

"Oh, no," Jo Ella said dully. "She—"

"Yes, she did," Avis insisted tearfully. "She pulled out that gun and she shot him, with that little boy looking on and just screaming—"

"My God." Jo Ella felt a chill go through her. "My God, when did this happen? Have the police been called? What—"

"No, no, no one knows about it yet and I just don't know what's going to happen to that poor baby. . . ."

Cam was slowly pulling the material of her blouse out of her waistband, and Jo Ella covered the phone and turned to him urgently. "Cam, something terrible has happened. There's been a shooting—"

Cam gave her a patient, peculiarly amused look and then took the telephone from her. He hoisted himself up on the counter and spoke casually into the receiver. "Hi, Ma. So old Marshall finally bit the big one, did he? I knew it was only a matter of time before that bastard got his just desserts. . . ." Jo Ella stared at him, horrified, but he remained implacable. "The kid? Oh, he'll probably grow up with an Oedipus complex and turn out to be some kind of Boston strangler or something—that is, if he doesn't go catatonic on us and spend the rest of his young years in a psycho ward. . . .

Oh, don't worry about her, she'll get off. The ones with the big chests always do. . . ." Jo Ella couldn't believe this. He was actually grinning about it. "Hell, Ma, I wish you wouldn't get so upset about these things—you know how your blood pressure is. I mean, you take this stuff entirely too seriously." Jo Ella fell back a step, incredulous, staring at him. Cam glanced at her, not even paying attention to what his mother was saying on the other end. The low light of desire began to kindle in his eyes. "Well, that's just fine, but right now I've got to get off the phone and make some serious love to my lady. You take it easy now. 'Bye."

Jo Ella backed away from him, eyes wide and mouth open, as Cam sprang lightly down from the counter and came toward her. "I—I can't believe," she gasped out as his hands fell lightly upon her waist, "what you just said to your mother!"

Cam pressed his lips against her neck. "Why? She knows we're sleeping together. She probably knew it before we did. God, you taste magnificent."

Jo Ella placed her hands on his shoulders, struggling away from him. "She was upset, Cam, with every right to be! How could you take it so casually, how could you be so cruel? You should go over there, you should—"

Cam lifted his face thoughtfully, then admitted with a rueful twist of his brow, "Yeah, I guess I could have been a little more understanding. She was kind of upset. But"—he lifted one shoulder philosophically—"I've told her before there's nothing I can do about it. If it starts to get too heavy for her, all she has to do is change the channel."

"There most certainly is something—" And then Jo

Ella froze, staring at him. "Change the..." Her hands dropped slowly from Cam's shoulders, her eyes widening with the dawning of a horrible suspicion. "You mean..."

Cam ducked his head to hide his grin, but his shoulders were already shaking with his chuckles. "A soap opera," he said into her neck, and his arms wrapped her tightly to prevent the blows of outrage he could sense coming.

But Jo Ella was too stunned to be angry, too relieved to be insulted. All this time she had been listening with such intense concern to the trials and tribulations of the Avis Scott neighbors, involving herself in their trouble, offering helpful advice and astute predictions—and all this time it had been no more than a soap opera! She could only stare at him in astonishment.

Cam lifted his head, trying to control the mirth dancing in his eyes, and he apologized meekly, "My mother leads a dull life."

Then there was nothing to do but laugh as he was laughing, and they clung to each other helplessly until laughter turned to playfulness and playfulness evolved naturally into arousal and arousal into passion—until Jo Ella's skirt was lying in a pool around her ankles and Cam's trousers were unfastened and Cam lifted her into his arms, murmuring, "I'll make dinner later...."

They never did get around to dinner that night. They made love and they drank champagne until restless or playful urges brought them together again. They explored every fantasy and every unspoken need, they teased and they tantalized and then they let their eyes and their touches burn relentless truths into each other's souls. They took each other gently and with sensual delight, they took each other with wild abandon and selfish greed. They knew each other's mind and body and they could not get enough. It was as though that night, in its playfully sensuous beginnings, had escalated into a culmination of all that had gone before. It was as though they were trying to store one night of love against hard times to come, or reaching one last desperate time for things not yet fulfilled—as though they knew, somehow, that the time was coming when what they had shared these last weeks, beautiful as it had been, would no longer be enough.

It was exhaustion, and perhaps a bit too much champagne, that forced their bodies at last into quiescence. Jo Ella lay with her head low on Cam's chest, one leg between his, her arm across his abdomen. His flesh was damp and pulsing steadily with the beat of his heart beneath her cheek. Cam's hand stroked her tangled hair, slowly, lethargically, his other hand spread quietly over her hips. She was physically replete, but there was still that restlessness within Jo Ella, a vague and undefined need. She did not want to go to sleep for fear of missing him. It seemed the more they were together the more she wanted of him, and there was never an end to it. It had never been like this for Jo Ella before.

She said at last, unable to raise her voice above a husky murmur, "Are you happy for me?"

"Darling, I'm in ecstasy." His voice was low and drowsy, a contented drawl.

"No, I mean about my job."

His lazy chuckle rumbled beneath her ear. "That, too."

Joe Ella turned her face to look at him. "I was beginning to think," she said carefully, "that I might not be able to find a job in Dallas. What if I hadn't? What if I had had to leave the city, or even go to another state?"

Cam's hand paused in its stroking motions for only a minute, then resumed again. His voice was casual, but she could sense his alertness. "Then that's what you would have done," he answered. He was speaking to the opposite wall.

Jo Ella felt something tighten in her stomach. It could have been disappointment, or it could have been anger at her own helplessness. It could have been fear. Still, after all they had shared, there was something standing between them. Still he held back from her. It hurt.

"I didn't want to," she whispered. And then with sudden urgency, "I didn't want to leave Dallas, I didn't want to leave you. I want to stay here with you and—"

"Hush." Swiftly, gently, he silenced her. He slipped his hand beneath her arms and pulled her upward, settling her head on his shoulder. "You don't have to say those things to me, Joey," he insisted quietly. "No promises, no commitments, that's the way it's always been between us. I won't hold you."

Jo Ella curled her hand against his chest as though to contain her own impotence; she swallowed back the pain his words had caused. Still he did not want her. Still he could not give himself completely to her keeping—and she knew why.

It was with this despair that Jo Ella fell into a restless sleep, and it was perhaps because of that—or it could have been the champagne—that the nightmares came.

She awoke on a strangled cry, with tears streaming down her face and a cold sheen of perspiration bathing her body, and it was Cam's hands she was trying to pull away from. It was his wrists she held and struggled against, and his face that was above her, and he said soothingly, "all right...all right...I'm going to let you go now. Are you awake? Wake up, Joey...."

His fingers slowly uncurled from about her shoulders and he sat back cautiously, watching her. She dragged in a gasping breath and brought her trembling hands to her wet cheeks, pressing them there, trying to contain the remnants of horror within her own mind or perhaps trying to reassure herself that it was over, that this was real and not the medicinal smell of hospital rooms and the metronomic bleeping of a monitor that burned through her brain. There was shame and there was terror because for one awful moment it had been as though Cam had been able to see into her dream, to know her guilt and her fear. "Oh, God," she whispered hoarsely, trying to calm her shaking breath. "It's been a long time since—" She gulped for air. "Since that happened, I—"

"No, it hasn't," Cam said calmly beside her. His hand gently tucked a strand of hair behind her ear. "You've had nightmares almost every night since I've been sleeping with you—never bad enough for me to wake you up, and you don't remember them in the morning, but you cry in your sleep." She lowered her hands slowly from her face and looked at him. Her eyes had adjusted to the room's twilight, and Cam's face was very sober. "I think," he said quietly, "It's time you talked about it, Joey."

Cam's eyes were tender and steady in the dark, his gentle touch on her shoulder soothing. Jo Ella knew he was right. It was time for the final barrier to come down between them, for she could not go on with the burden of her secret any longer. There would be no tenderness in his eyes when Jo Ella finished her story, but she could not hide herself from him anymore.

She got out of bed and walked slowly to the closet in the dark, pulling out a robe to cover her nakedness. Cam sat on the bed behind her, saying nothing, simply waiting. After a long time she began to speak.

"Six months," she said quietly. "He was in the hospital for six months. No one understood, really, what was happening. He just kept getting worse. We did everything we could, but he refused to heal. But at the beginning, while he was mobile, he was one of those rare patients that everybody loved." A smile curved in her voice. "He would go to the wards and visit with the other patients, the pediatrics and the surgical patients. We used to joke about having to track him down. He did magic tricks for the kids and cartoon character voices—you know, Donald Duck and Mickey Mouse. He was good, too. And he always had some really raunchy jokes to tell the nurses." She almost laughed, remembering. "It was the high point of every shift to see what joke Bobby had come up with that day. And even—" her voice fell, though she tried not to let it—"even after things got bad for him, he always had that joke...." And now her voice was almost a whisper. "Only sometimes he couldn't remember the punch line...."

She caught her breath, she steeled her nerves. She

had to go on. "His body just kept deteriorating. He had allergies to the medication and post-op infections, and he wouldn't recover. He lost so much weight that his heart couldn't keep up with the vital functions and started to weaken under the stress." She was reciting medical facts now. It was easier that way. "His kidneys failed; he contracted pneumonia and a bad staph infection. He just wouldn't get better. Finally the doctor wrote on his chart, 'The patient is dying—and we don't know why.'" Cam knew all of this, it had come out in the trial. But she needed to say it anyway. "So he died, and we brought him back." Her fists began to close at her sides. "His heart stopped and we started it again—and again and again and again. And every time—" here her voice caught, but she fought it determinedly—"every time there was a little less of that spark in his eyes, a little more despair, and finally when he looked at us it was as though he hated us. He said—" her voice fell to almost a whisper—"he begged us... he said, 'Why won't you let me go?'"

Jo Ella had been standing at the window, looking blankly out. Now she half turned back toward the room, her hands clasped rigidly before her, but she still could not look at Cam. And still Cam said nothing. "His parents," she went on, steadier now, "begged the doctors to take him off life support. He was suffering so. There was nothing we could do. His heart was failing, his kidneys were gone, he had no intestines left. There was nothing we could do but let the machines breathe for him and take over his body functions. His wife—it was destroying her. She came to me, begging me to do something, to talk to the doctors, to do something . . . to let Bobby die. And Bobby . . . there was such hoplessness in his eyes," she said softly. "Such despair trapped within that suffering shell of a body that we refused to let die. I used to come and sit with him, even when I wasn't on duty. I don't know why. There was nothing I could do. He would cry, and he would hold my hand. He was so weak he could hardly talk, but he kept begging me over and over, 'Let me go . . . please, just let me go. . . .'"

And now she took a breath. She turned to look at Cam, very calm now, unafraid. "So one night I was sitting with him, and he was crying and holding my hand, and his eyes were so trapped, so hopeless . . . I reached over and I switched off the monitor. Then I disconnected the life support systems. And I sat there and I held his hand until he wasn't holding my hand any longer. . . ." Her eyes grew vague, taking her back to that night, to the horror beyond it, to the peace that had settled upon it. "I'm not sorry," she whispered brokenly. "I don't want you to hate me, but I'm not sorry. I would do it again, even though I know it was wrong, I would . . ."

She had to take a breath. She had to look at him now, to face him with the final truth and accept the consequences. His face was shadowed in the dark. She said, as clearly and as evenly as possible, her hands twisted tightly before her, "I—lied on the stand. I told them what—what the hospital attorneys wanted me to say, that I was—too tired, and too upset, to notice that the monitor wasn't on when I came in, that the life-support systems weren't working. . . ." Her fists tightened and she felt the cut of her nails on her palms, but she had to go on, firmly, honestly, because she owed him this much. "I lied about it, Cam, because they told me to—and because I couldn't go to prison... because I would have died in prison...." Her breath caught with a sound like a sob. The truth sounded ugly, and hateful, but it was the truth and she had to tell it the best way she knew how. She had to tell it and be unashamed of it—and she wasn't ashamed, not of what she had done. She wasn't sorry. It came back to her, the gentle lightening of Bobby's grip upon her hand, the soft, tired exhalation of his final breath, the peace that rested at last in his face, and she felt a part of that peace steal over her. She lifted her chin slightly, her muscles relaxing, and she said again, very softly, "I'm not sorry. I set him free, and I'm not sorry."

It seemed the silence rang within the room forever. Jo Ella made her eyes at last focus upon Cam's figure, but she could see nothing of his face in the dark. It was as well. She could not bear to see the hatred there, the revulsion, the shock. And then Cam said, very quietly, "Joey, I know. I've known all along." And he stretched his hand out to her. "Being you, what else could you have done?"

She came to him, haltingly; she felt his fingers touch her, and then she stumbled into his arms. He wrapped himself around her, holding her, comforting her, giving her the warmth of his skin and the strength of his arms, and she clutched at him, pressing herself into him, desperately holding on to him. The joy, the peace and contentment that filled her then was transcendental, all-encompassing, unshakable. A burden shared was a burden halved, but Cam's unquestioning understanding of the most dreadful decision of her life was more than just an easing of her pain. It was the opening of the door that set her spirit free, and Jo Ella thought that "love" was a pale word to describe what she felt for Cam then.

But for the moment, it would have to do.

Chapter Eleven

It was the day before Thanksgiving. Jo Ella had decided to visit Mary, even though she knew they would all see each other tomorrow, mostly because she was ashamed of having been to see the baby only once, in the hospital, but partly because she simply needed to get away.

Jo Ella had pretended to be asleep this morning while Cam dressed for work. She was ashamed of the dark confessions of the night before, frightened of what she might see in his eyes. Those gentle words, "I've known all along," had had the power to save her floundering spirit last night. Cam knew, and Cam understood. Cam forgave. But did he really? Would she see the truth in his eyes this morning? Would she see accusation and disappointment there now, disgust and mistrust?

Cam would not let her get away with the ruse. He stood over the bed until his shadow was a weight bearing down on her, and Jo Ella could not help stirring restlessly beneath it. "It's not working, Joey," he said, and she could hear a lazy smile in his voice. "I know you're awake. Open your eyes."

She turned over slowly and looked at him. He sat down on the edge of the bed, smoothing her hair away from her eyes. There was nothing in his face but tenderness. He looked at her for a long, long time, his hands cupping her face. Then he said quietly, "Don't ever do that again, Joey. Don't ever try to hide the truth from me, don't ever think I won't understand. Don't ever forget that I know you better than anyone else in the world, and that"—he leaned forward and kissed her lips gently—"I love you."

He loved her. Cam loved her and he understood, and Jo Ella thought her heart would fill to bursting at that moment. Something swelled inside her and transcended the narrow confines of her own emotions; it seemed to fall with a golden glow over both of them, wrapping them together in one moment of clear and untrammeled unity. Something was released inside her that was more powerful than a painful secret, more encompassing than her own needs. She felt free for the first time in her entire life.

And it was perhaps the restlessness of joy that drove Jo Ella from the apartment that morning. She felt unfettered and light; she wanted to run down the street and shout to everyone she met that she was loved and that she loved, she wanted to do something wildly insane like performing pirouettes in the middle of downtown traffic. She knew for the first time in her life exactly what she wanted. She wanted to live with Cam in his spacious, window-filled house on the edge of a pecan orchard and be his lover, his wife, the mother of his children, forever. And for the first time in her life, it really seemed possible. She felt light enough to fly.

But instead Jo Ella did something conventional and conservative, the kind of thing Cam would approve of. She went to the shopping mall and bought an eight-piece layette set of pale yellow fleece for the new addition to the family, and she went to visit Cam's sister-in-law.

The first thing Jo Ella noticed was the three children playing outside, and that alarmed her because one of them, at least, should have been in school. Then she remembered the Thanksgiving holidays and resigned herself to spending a hectic few minutes wrestling Mary's attention from the children instead of the leisurely morning she had planned, admiring the baby. Tricycles, Big Wheels, Tonka trucks and various other modes of transportation were scattered all over the driveway, and Jo Ella had to park in the street. The two oldest boys were engaged in a violent laser pistol fight and did not even look up as Jo Ella came up the driveway. The three-year-old was curled up with a box of Cheerios in the boxwood that lined the front entrance, and he looked up at Jo Ella with frightened, soulful eyes. The front door was standing wide open.

Jo Ella had never known Mary to be so disorganized. It didn't seem her style to leave the front door open while the children ran in and out, or to let her youngest eat dry cereal out of a box in the front yard. He was filthy, too, his face streaked with tears and dirt, his shirt torn. For that matter, Jo Ella had never known Mary to let the children play unsupervised, but she philosophized that a new baby brought lots of changes to an otherwise orderly household, and Mary was probably finding that she had her hands more than full.

Jo Ella leaned down to the little boy, smiling. "Hi, there. Where's Mommy?"

He looked up at her soberly. Jo Ella could hear, faintly, from the open front door, the angry squall of an infant. She realized that the baby had been crying all along, but the sound had simply blended into the background noise until she got close enough to define it. It didn't seem like Mary, either, to let her baby cry for so long at such a furious, unattended pitch, but Jo Ella tried not to be disturbed. There was such a thing as a colicky infant, she knew.

The little boy said at last, unblinking, "Sleeping."

Jo Ella hardly thought that was likely, certainly not with a baby screaming in the background, but she smiled at him and went inside.

The house was a disaster, a testament to what three children could do in a short time if left to their own devices. Toys were scattered from hallway to front door, as well as the contents of someone's dresser drawer. The coffee table was overturned, a figurine smashed on the fireplace. There were jelly smears on the window and a box of cookies emptied in a steady stream across the floor. And the baby was crying. Jo Ella was shocked to see Mary's house in such condition, but she tried not to be alarmed. She told herself it was a busy morning, that was all, and could she, Jo Ella, keep up with three small boys and an infant and still find time to clean her house? But the truth was that Jo Ella knew, from the moment she stepped into the room, that something was wrong, very wrong, and the knowledge tightened like a cold fist in her chest with every passing second, with every renewed scream of the furious infant.

She put the package she was carrying on the lamp table by the door and called cautiously, "Mary?"

No reply.

Jo Ella stepped into the room, moving carefully over Matchbox cars and cookie crumbs, and called louder, "Mary, it's Jo Ella. Where are you?"

There was no response except the high-pitched, raucous scream of the baby. The house seemed to breathe an aura of stillness, of desertion, of something very, very wrong.

Jo Ella could hear her pulse pounding in her ears as she crossed the room. She moved slowly, even though her brain urged her to hurry, hurry... but she couldn't seem to get the message to her feet. She called out again and again—only the ceaseless, sirenlike wail of the infant answered her. It was tangible now, something she could taste and feel all around her, pushing at her, clamoring at her—danger, disaster, a good thing gone wrong....

She turned into the hallway and the crying of the baby was closer now, setting her teeth on edge, making her want to scream out loud, but her mouth was too dry even to call out. She passed the boys' room, and a glimpse inside told her that, except for a jumble of toys and clothes, it was empty. A bathroom was littered with wet towels and toilet paper. A bedroom door was closed and Jo Ella's knock was weak, then strengthened by the persistent cry of the deprived baby. There was no answer. She called out. Her sweaty hand turned the doorknob.

Mary was lying on the unmade bed in her bathrobe, and at first the relief that swept through Jo Ella was palpable. From the window came the sounds of children playing and fighting in the front yard, from the hallway came the never-tiring cry of the baby. Jo Ella wanted to shout at Mary, to shake her and demand what in the world she thought she was doing, taking a nap at this time of day with her children running wild and her baby screaming for attention.... All of that passed, of course, in only a matter of seconds. Jo Ella was too much a professional not to know what had happened. And Mary was still, pale and lifeless.

Jo Ella went quickly to the bed and shook Mary's arm, calling to her. The body bounced on the bed with the force of her grip, but Mary did not open her eyes. Something dim and far away inside Jo Ella was whispering, *Oh, God, Oh, God, no, don't let it be*...even as the professional side of her noted the cold, clammy texture of the woman's skin and her fingers felt frantically for a pulse. Her own heart was roaring so loudly in her ears that she couldn't concentrate. She pressed her fingers to Mary's neck, her cheek close to her parted lips. The throb beneath Jo Ella's fingers was faint and thready, and she thought she felt a dim whisper of air against her face. The baby cried in the background, the children played outside, and Jo Ella's head was roaring.

Jo Ella shook Mary again and slapped her lightly on both cheeks, but there was no response. She looked frantically around the room and then she saw it, an empty medicine bottle and an overturned water glass on the night table.

For just a second Jo Ella fell victim to that paralyzing

sensation low in her solar plexus that was akin to having the breath knocked out of her from a fall. She had known it, she had known what must have happened from the beginning, but there was something about seeing it, seeing the concrete evidence within the reach of her fingers, the ugly, harsh finality of the empty medicine bottle.

She snatched up the bottle, but her hands were shaking so badly that for a second she couldn't read the label. Valium. It leaped out at her all at once. Valium, three grains, number twenty... Had she taken all twenty pills? Had the bottle been full or had there been only a few left? Was that water dripping all over the night stand or alcohol? How long ago, how much, and why... why... *why*?

Suddenly something snapped within Jo Ella—fury, outrage, despair, impotence. She grabbed Mary by the shoulders, half lifting her off the bed, shaking her hard and screaming, "Damn you! Damn you for doing this!" Mary's head snapped limply back and forth, her hair tangling in her eyes and her mouth, and Jo Ella was filled with a white-hot rage, an instinctive fight for the value of human life, a sense of helplessness and fury that anyone should treat it so lightly. "You're not going to die, do you hear me?" Jo Ella slapped her lightly, again and again, across the face, still shaking her, screaming at her. "You have no right—you're not going to just walk out.... I'm not going to let you do this, do you hear me? *You're not going to die*!"

Behind her another hysterical, high-pitched voice joined with the hiccoughing wail of the baby. "You're hitting my mama! Stop it, stop it, *stop it*!" but Jo Ella did not turn around. She continued shaking Mary and yelling at her, and she did not know whether she held out some dim hope that her words might penetrate or whether what motivated her it was just the need to shout all of her outrage and fear and desperation. And finally, at last, Mary opened her eyes a crack and her lips moved.

"Leave me alone," she muttered. "Just want to rest...so tired..." And then her eyes closed again.

Jo Ella let her limp form drop. Perspiration was beading on her forehead and dampening her collar, and she was breathing hard. It wasn't over yet—Mary was still drifting out of semiconsciousness. Jo Ella let the efficient, professional side of her take over while the mad demon that had screamed and fought for Mary's life seethed just below the surface; she snatched the bedside telephone off the hook and punched out the emergency number.

It was a blur from then on. The ambulance was on its way. The children were screaming and the baby was crying, but Jo Ella could not leave Mary. She somehow dragged her off the bed and got her to her feet, and Jo Ella felt every muscle in her back tear beneath the effort. She dragged her around the room, a few inches at a time, for most of the time Mary was dead weight. She talked to Mary, never once remembering what she said. The ambulance seemed to take hours; in fact, it was there in less than ten minutes. By the time the efficient uniformed paramedics arrived, Jo Ella's body was a drenched and aching mass and Mary seemed no closer to consciousness than she had been at first. The nurse in Jo Ella helped the paramedics get Mary onto the stretcher and set up the IV, remembered to send the medicine bottle and the name of Mary's doctor with them and calmed the children absently and automatically, and the woman inside her was screaming with the high-pitched pain of the blaring siren as the ambulance sped away.

The neighbors came out. One of them ushered the three boys into her house to play while giving Jo Ella shocked, helpless looks; another came inside to attend to the baby, who had not stopped screaming all this time. Jo Ella dialed Cam's number and told him in crisp, efficient sentences to what hospital Mary had been taken. Afterward she did not even remember the sound of his voice or whether he had asked questions; she only remembered that he sounded calm and competent and in control while everything inside her was slowly shredding and being scattered to the wind.

The baby had stopped crying. The neighbor, a young woman with short blond hair and calm eyes, brought Jo Ella a cup of coffee and made her sit down in the cool light of the patio. "The baby was just hungry, that's all," she explained with a gentle smile, and Jo Ella nodded dully. She remembered when she and Mary had sat in these very chairs, looking out over the lawn and refereeing fights and talking about their lives. She should have known. *She should have known*....

The cup clattered against the saucer as Jo Ella lifted it to drink. She had to get hold of herself. This was routine for any emergency ward in the city. Jo Ella was a professional, she knew how to handle things like this. *It's just so senseless,* she though in dull despair. *So terribly senseless.*

"She said she was tired," Jo Ella said softly, staring into her coffee cup. The young woman looked at her alertly. "She said she just wanted to rest."

The neighbor, whose name Jo Ella was never to learn, looked away uncomfortably, not knowing what to say. No one knew how to deal with something like this. It was shocking and it was embarrassing on the most primitive level, and it was more than a little frightening. It was something that should be hushed up and glanced at askance and quickly turned away from, perhaps because within everyone there was an ugly recognition of the act and its motives... because everyone had their own personal border, fuzzy at times and starkly clear at others, the limit over which one more step would mean escape... because everyone had been or would be at the point Mary was this morning, and there was secret shame, and a feeling of guilt over not knowing whether or not they would have the courage to turn away from that next step.

Jo Ella finished her coffee, then, drawing on inner resources of strength, as was her custom to get through the things that had to be done, she called Avis and asked her to come and get the boys. Caring for the baby would be her own responsibility. She and the kind young neighbor silently and methodically began to straighten up the house. Before she left, the young woman went across the street and brought home the boys, who were much subdued by now, and Jo Ella washed them and changed their clothes and helped them pack for the visit to Grandma's. She calmly answered their questions and assured them that their mother would be fine and come home soon, and she did not know whether or not she was lying. At that point she supposed it did not matter. The neighbor showed Jo Ella where the formula and diapers were kept and assured her she would be right next door if there were any problems, then left with a kind smile and a reassuring pat on the hand as Avis drove up.

Avis showed her true mettle in a real-life crisis. On the telephone Jo Ella had told her simply that Mary was ill and had to be taken to the hospital; Avis did not fold when Jo Ella told her now the true details of the incident. There was shock and horror and swift concern, but no hysterics. Jo Ella had noticed before that Avis seemed to have more control over the boys than either of their parents, and that grandmotherly competence was in evidence now. Jo Ella was relieved not to have to worry about either the children or their grandmother.

Avis got the boys in the car and stayed and talked a few more minutes, quietly, with Jo Ella. Jo Ella did not remember what was said. Inane reassurances, probably, senseless questions. When one of the boys piped up from the back seat, "Are we going to have turkey tomorrow, Grandma?" Jo Ella saw a quick flash of tears in Avis's eyes, and then there was nothing more to say.

Jo Ella was left alone in the hauntingly silent house with the sleeping baby, and she felt a knot of fear settle just below her breastbone, a tight band that wouldn't go away no matter how many deep breaths she took. She wandered through the house, neatening things that had already been straightened, marveling over how normal it looked. No one would guess that only hours ago the most crucial battle of any life had been fought here, the decision point had been reached and passed and nothing in this quiet, homey, normal-looking house would ever be the same again.

When the phone rang, Jo Ella could not make herself answer it. It shrilled again and again, demanding attention, and the baby began to whimper. Her feet had turned to blocks of ice, but somehow she crossed the room.

"She's out of danger," Cam said, and Jo Ella released her breath in one long stream, her weak knees buckling under her and causing her to grope for the sofa. "They're going to keep her here for a few days... Burt hasn't been able to see her yet."

Jo Ella nodded. It was standard procedure. She told Cam about the arrangements she had made for the children and that she would stay with the baby.

"I'm going to bring Burt home as soon as I can," Cam said. He sounded drained and tired. "He's about to break." There was a silence, and Jo Ella closed her eyes against the sudden sweeping pain that reached out to Cam, that wanted to hold him and be held by him, to comfort each other with the solid reassurance of their life in the wake of so near a brush with death. He said quietly, "Are you all right, Joey?"

Jo Ella had to swallow hard before she could answer. Even then her voice was little above a whisper. "Yes. Yes, I'm fine. You take care of Burt. I'll be here when you get back."

She hung up the phone carefully and let the relief flow through her. Mary was all right. She wasn't going to die. She wasn't going to walk out on four children and the man who loved her—not this time, not while

Jo Ella was here to watch. There was a fierce satisfaction in that, a victory hard won. But it was only one battle in an endless war, and no one could say what the outcome of the next one would be. And that tight band of fear just below Jo Ella's heart would not go away.

She busied herself with mundane matters, warming baby formula, making plans, taking care of the future. She would have to call her mother. Obviously, the Thanksgiving reunion was off. Burt could not be left here to take care of the baby by himself. Jo Ella doubted if he had ever changed a diaper in his life. No, she would have to take the baby home with her, and babies came complete with a lot of equipment. She kept her mind occupied by making a list as she changed the baby and brought her into the living room to feed her.

She sat in the big rocking chair before the fireplace where, no doubt, Mary had sat many hours, the small, sweet-smelling bundle cradled in her arms and making greedy smacking sounds against the nipple of the bottle. Jo Ella had handled many babies, and she had always enjoyed delivery room or nursery duty, just as she had diligently avoided the pediatric or newborn ICU assignments. The suffering of infants was one thing Jo Ella knew instinctively she was not equipped to deal with. But never had her maternal instincts been aroused like this, never had she felt so powerfully that sweep of wonder and delight that comes from holding a bundle of newly created life in one's arms, feeling it move and breathe and suckle and promise all the wild imaginings of the future in its tiny form. Suddenly she was swept by a wave of yearning and fierce protectiveness so powerful that it shook her, she wanted to hold the baby tight against her chest and never let her go. A tiny eye blinked in surprise as one of Jo Ella's tears splashed on her cheek, and Jo smiled through the helplessness of confusion and pain that was wracking her. "How could she do it?" she whispered. "How could she want to leave a beautiful thing like you?"

But the child, sucking contentedly on her bottle, had no answer.

JO ELLA'S TRAINED EYE saw in Burt all the symptoms of a man on the verge of collapse. His eyes were stunned, his face haggard, his hair rumpled. He walked with the uncertain, lurching gait of someone swimming his way upward through waves of shock, and when he sank into a chair by the door, he didn't say anything. He simply sat there, looking around him as though wondering where he was and how he had gotten there.

Jo Ella took one look at Burt, then asked Cam quietly, "Did they give him anything at the hospital?"

Cameron shook his head, and though Jo Ella, through the events of the day, felt a natural repulsion for the use of drugs even in alcoholic form, she went to the bar and poured Burt a large brandy.

Burt accepted the glass wordlessly, and Cameron sat down near his brother, keeping a cautious eye on him as he told Jo Ella, "Mary's going to be all right." He spoke soothingly, more for Burt's benefit than for Jo Ella's. "They're going to keep her under observation for a few days and she'll get psychiatric therapy, but the doctor isn't worried. They see this as more of a cry for help than a serious"—he hesitated over the word—"attempt."

Burt took a shuddering breath, then glanced at Jo Ella and for the first time seemed to notice her presence. "Thank God you were here," he said. His voice was hoarse and strained. He took another deep drink of the brandy, and then he dropped his head slowly, resting it on the palm of one hand; he closed his eyes against the agony Jo Ella could see welling up inside him. "God, I don't understand," he whispered, then, more fiercely, "I don't understand." He looked suddenly at Cam. "She never said anything to me, she never complained. I knew this was rough on her and I offered to get her some help, but she wouldn't hear of it, she wanted to do it all herself and she never said anything to me.... Why didn't she talk to me?" His eyes dropped wearily back to the glass. "God, if only I had known, if we could have talked.... I don't understand," he said wearily. "I just don't understand."

Jo Ella knew the stages Burt was going through. There would be disbelief and confusion, then anger, and at last, she hoped, a form of acceptance, much like the stages of mourning. And he had to go through it all by himself. There was nothing Jo Ella could do to help him.

She got up and knelt beside him, laying a hand lightly on his arm. "Burt," she said softly, "I'm going to take the baby home with me. The boys are with your mother. I don't want you to worry about anything—Mary needs all your attention right now, and you have to take care of yourself, too. Try to eat something tonight. Cam will stay with you"—she glanced at Cam for assent, and he gave an imperceptible nod—"for as long as you need him, okay? You just take care of yourself."

Jo Ella could see his lips tighten and knew he was trying not to cry. He patted her hand in gratitude and nodded wordlessly.

Obviously glad to have something useful to do, Cameron helped Jo Ella pack the bassinet, diaper bag and extra formula into the car, then secured the car seat and helped her strap the still-sleeping infant inside. The strain was showing in his face, and when their eyes met the bleakness of the question passed from one to the other, *Why*? and the equally empty answer, *I don't know... I just don't know.* He did not kiss her, and not one word passed between them. There was nothing that could be said. He clasped her hand for just a moment as she got into the car, and it was an attempt to gain strength as much as give it. He stood on the lawn and watched her drive away, and Jo Ella caught a glimpse of his wearily slumped shoulders through the rearview mirror as he turned to go back into the house.

THE DEMANDS of getting a baby settled in the house kept Jo Ella busy for a few hours and kept her mind from racing. She gave herself over to the little pleasures of bathing, dressing and feeding little Tiffany, of arranging the bassinet in a warm corner of the living room near the bedroom door and of laying out her tiny, soft garments. She sat and rocked the baby long after Tiffany had drifted off into a well-fed sleep, simply because it felt so good to have something warm and alive in her arms. And over and over Jo Ella kept thinking, *I don't understand. Mary had so much. Why did she want to leave it all? How could she give it up?* But deep inside Jo Ella did know, she did understand, and that was why that persistent ache of fear in her chest would not subside.

Cam came in just after four A.M. Jo Ella had just gotten back to bed after feeding the baby, but she had not slept at all during the night. She lay there and watched Cam undress in the diffuse light of the muted yellow lamp she had left burning in the living room, and she ached for him and herself, and for the fragility of life and the fleeting nature of time everywhere. Cam's body was cold as he slid into bed beside her, but she did not mind the touch of his hand on her hip beneath her nightgown. She moved toward him, drawing him into her arms, curling one leg over his hips and around his waist. His heart beat steady and sure against her ear, and she felt the long, slow intake of his breath as he pressed himself into her, deep inside her. That way they stayed, clinging to each other wordlessly, motionlessly, for the few hours of refuge the night would allow them.

Chapter Twelve

Though "normal" was not a word that could ever be applied to the situation, not in the present or in the future, Cam's and Jo Ella's lives settled down within the next few days into a routine of sorts, and it was not an unpleasant one. Perhaps it was no more than the relief that was natural when tragedy brushes close by but leaves one's own life basically untouched, perhaps it was a renewed gratitude and sense of value for each other. Perhaps it was the simple joy that a baby, with all its inconveniences and trials, could bring into a house. Jo Ella knew that those days with Cam and his infant niece would remain forever among the most treasured memories of her life. Perhaps it was because she sensed, even then, how fragile it all was. How easily it could all slip away.

Tiffany stayed with them for a week. Mary was out of the hospital in three days, but her therapist advised a period of quiet recuperation before she moved back into a fully occupied household again. Jo Ella and Cam took the baby for a visit once, and Mary seemed tired, a little sad, but the awful tension that had once been in her eyes was not so noticeable anymore. She did not want them to take the baby away again, and her eyes brimmed with love for her daughter and regret for all she had almost lost. But Burt gently reminded her of the doctor's advice, and Mary voiced no further objections. She trusted the care of her baby to a registered nurse and a loving uncle, and she was taking no chances with the tensions that had pushed her to a brink from which there almost had been no turning back. Jo Ella left, much impressed with Mary's chances for a full recovery but still strangely, uneasily depressed.

Burt was taking time off to stay with Mary, and Cam was keeping the business together. The boys were still with Avis and, from all reports, getting a crash course in manners and discipline to which they were reacting very favorably. Everyone was handling the stress quite well and even seeming to emerge from it stronger for the experience, but that nagging little ache of uncertainty in Jo Ella's chest never quite seemed to disappear completely.

Cam stepped into the role of surrogate father naturally and easily, just as Jo Ella knew he would. He never missed an opportunity to cuddle or play with the baby, and they bickered like a married couple over his tendency to overstimulate the infant, especially after feeding. He came home loaded with oversized and inappropriate toys, and Jo Ella teased him that his living room was beginning to look like the display counter at F.A.O. Schwartz, at which he only grinned and gently scooped the sleeping infant out of her bassinet. "It brings out the kid in me, I guess," he admitted, "to have a baby around." He looked at Tiffany, who stubbornly refused to wake up, with undisguised affection. "She's a good baby, isn't she? Hardly ever cries."

"A rare characteristic," Jo Ella assured him, beginning to stack his latest contribution to the stuffed animal menagerie on top of the stereo. "They're not all like that, believe me. And besides—" she shot him a wry glance—"when she does cry, you've got to admit she chooses the best possible time."

He grinned, remembering the night before, when Tiffany had begun to demand her ten o'clock feeding just as they were approaching the most crucial point in some very intense lovemaking. "Admit it," he challenged. "You love it. It's fun having a baby around the house, and you know it."

Jo Ella's smile softened, and she paused to stroke a wisp of raven-black hair that curled over the sleeping baby's forehead. "Sure," she agreed. "But," she had to add sensibly, "I don't think it would be quite as much fun, for either of us, if we didn't know we had to give her back at the end of the week."

"Maybe," Cam agreed enigmatically, and bent to replace Tiffany, who had not stirred once, back into the bassinet.

"Really, Cam," Jo Ella exclaimed in exasperation, staring, with her hands on her hips, at the outrageous display of toys lining the wall and spilling onto the floor. "You've got to learn to control yourself. What are you going to do with all these things when Tiffany leaves? Burt and Mary don't have room for them—they have three generations of hand-me-downs to get through first. It's very wasteful," she reprimanded him.

"Oh, I don't know." He straightened up with a lingering smile for the baby. "I'll have kids of my own someday." The gentle meaning in his eyes was clear and subtly inviting, not threatening or implying, merely edging up to a truth they both knew they would have to deal with soon. "I'll save them until then."

But that little knot of uneasiness in Jo Ella's chest intensified, and she had to turn away.

Jo Ella's mother called, first to offer her sympathy and her help if it was needed, later to check on the progress of all concerned.

"Everything's fine, Mom," Jo Ella assured her. "Mary's out of the hospital and should be on her feet again soon."

"You're not having any trouble coping with that little one, are you?" Jo Ella's mother would have liked nothing better than to receive a desperate plea for help in the baby-sitting department.

Jo Ella smiled tolerantly. "I'm a nurse, Mom, remember? I'm doing just fine."

"Well..." her mother responded doubtfully, "there's a lot more to mothering than just nursing, Jo Ella. You've never had any real experience."

Jo Ella's patience was wearing thin. "Mother..."

"Oh, that reminds me." Her mother made a quick and judicious change of subject. "Some doctor has been calling here for you. I didn't want to give him Cam's number without asking you first, but I told him I would give you the message. Dr. Jordan?"

Jo Ella could hear her mother fumbling for the scrap of paper on which she had written the message. "Albert Jordan?" Her attention quickened.

"Yes, yes—that's right. Here it is. He left a number for you to call him—before December fifteenth, he said. It's a New York number," her mother added, somewhat in awe.

Albert Jordan. Jo Ella had worked with him two years ago on a brief assignment in Japan. He was a corporate physician who was transferred regularly to various parts of the world, and when they parted he had expressed interest in working with Jo Ella again. They had talked several times since, but none of his offers had appealed to Jo Ella at the time they were made. He could be calling just to check in with her, to let her know he was back in the States and to perhaps offer his sympathies on her recent troubles, but somehow Jo Ella did not think so. "Did he say what he wanted?" Jo Ella already had pen and paper in hand to copy down the number.

"No, just the telephone number." Jo Ella's mother read off the numbers and Jo Ella copied them down routinely, even though she had no intention of returning his call.

Jo Ella finished the conversation with her mother and did not think too much more about Albert Jordan. But later that day she called Kay Dobbins at the travel agency at which she was supposed to begin work and asked her if she could hold the position open for another week. She gave as her excuse the family crisis, although Jo Ella was pretty sure Tiffany would be back with her natural parents before she was scheduled to report for work. In fact, she did not really know why she made the call. She only knew that the tight anxiety that had been gnawing at her for the past week eased a little once she did it.

Cam insisted upon taking the two o'clock feeding, even though Jo Ella argued that he had to go to work every morning and needed his sleep more than she did. But Cam got out of bed at the first whimper, even though Jo Ella was already on her way to the kitchen for the formula, and gradually she began to understand. He was not doing it for her, but for himself. He needed the contact, the warmth and wonder of new life held in his arms in the midst of this dark and troublesome time just as much as Jo Ella did. And in the end they both got up for the middle-of-the-night feedings, one of them holding the baby while the other warmed the formula, each of them treasuring the still, reverent moments that reminded them there was hope even in the midst of tragedy. And afterward they would go to bed and make love with a quiet intensity, an almost desperate ferocity, that was their way of reaffirming their faith in life, of keeping at bay dark foes they could not even name.

In the early hours of one morning, Jo Ella reached for Cam and his pillow was cold. She turned over on her back, clutching the covers to her, opening her eyes to a fuzzy dark ceiling and trying to shake away the remnants of a nightmare. She had been dreaming about the hospital again. Only in her dream Bobby Williams's face had been replaced with Mary's, and two voices instead of one were pleading with her, "Let me go...." "I just want to rest...." "Please let me go...."

These were the worst times. These dark and empty hours of predawn when the mind was defenseless and nightmares could come true, when the soul was stripped bare and vulnerable to the horrors of life the waking mind would try to ignore. During the day they could keep it at bay with sunshine and routine, with jokes and smiles and the little pleasures and trials of everyday life. But the subconscious ruled the night and left them victims to dark truths, and then there was nothing to do but to creep out of bed and seek solace in the warmth and hope of one small life held for a brief time in their arms.

Cam was sitting in the rocking chair near the bassinet, feeding the baby. Jo Ella did not go to him but stood at the door of the bedroom, unwilling to disturb the moment. Never had anything looked so beautiful. Cam, wearing only his hastily pulled-on jeans, his hair rumpled and his face peaceful with the residue of sleep, awash in the amber glow of lamplight, holding the baby against his bare torso. One of his broad hands almost spanned the length of the child's body, yet there was such gentleness, such infinite care in the way he supported her in the crook of his arm and held the bottle for her with the other hand, that it took Jo Ella's breath away. There was something about a man half dressed and tender, holding a baby in his arms, that was both sexy and virile, vulnerable and strong, and it touched on a very primal level the woman within Jo Ella. It led her, in that moment, down paths fuzzy with the character of daydreams to a house at the edge of an orchard, earth and sky all around, bright laughter-filled days and tender early-morning hours. Would that be their baby he was holding in his arms in a few years? Would it be Jo Ella that he came home to at the end of a long day, would there be toys to trip over and querulous voices to greet him while dinner bubbled on the stove and his eyes filled with light when he saw her?

Or would Jo Ella, like Mary, one day look around at the walls closing in on her and just walk away, just turn her back on children and husband and home and all she loved and just walk and keep on walking....

Her vision had lost its focus; she did not realize that Cam had placed the sleeping baby gently back in the bassinet and he was watching her steadily, reading her mind. She knew he was reading her mind because when her eyes found his they were brooding, troubled, and the gentle light had gone out of them.

She smiled quickly. "Guess I overslept."

He opened his arms to her. "One lap, no waiting," he invited.

Jo Ella came to him, cuddling against his broad chest, letting his arms wrap her in security and soothe her troubles away. "Let's play a game," he suggested. "I'll be the analyst and you be the patient."

"Sounds kinky to me," murmured Jo Ella. His chest was warm and smooth beneath her cheek, his hands sure and firm across her hips and her back. His lips brushed her hair.

"So tell me, madam," he said persuasively in a deep German accent, "what seems to be the source of your distress?"

She giggled, curling her fist against the tight muscles of his breast, and he said quietly, "Nightmares again?"

Jo Ella took a tight breath that pushed against the band of anxiety in her chest. "Oh, Cam," she whispered. Cameron could feel her muscles tensing beneath his hands. "I just keep thinking there was something I could have done, I should have known what she was thinking and how she was feeling, I should have seen the signs. If I had been more sympathetic, or spent more time with her...."

"Shh." His fingers stroked her taut shoulder muscles, his lips touched her hair again. "You saved her life, Jo Ella. You were right there when it was important and you did all the right things. There was no way you could have known in advance. Burt lived with her and he didn't know. You did everything you could, and it was right."

You did everything you could... and it was right. How many times had she said those words to herself in a desperate attempt to exonerate herself from the responsibility of Bobby Williams's death? Could Cam understand how the two lives for which she had been responsible, Mary's and Bobby's, had entwined themselves in her mind? Could he understand that the emotions that had driven her in those desperate moments she had fought for Mary were somehow tangled up with the same ones that had made her turn off a switch in a dim hospital room almost a year ago? That she had fought more than just Mary's desperate action; she had fought rage at her own helplessness, and perhaps she had somehow thought that by saving Mary's life she could make up for the one she had let go.

"I think," Cameron said quietly, "you still have a little bit of guilt about Bobby Williams, and I think what happened with Mary only brought it to the surface. It was a shock to see that just because you've turned your back on your trained profession you can't necessarily avoid facing your own helplessness sometimes, and that even though you don't face it every day anymore there are still going to be lives depending on you, responsibilities you have to face.

"That's the human condition, Joey. We're all involved with other people and we're all responsible for them in some way or another—maybe not as dramatically as you were, but responsible nonetheless. The secret to living with that is in knowing your own limits... in knowing when to let go."

"Sometimes I don't know," she said slowly, tightly, "whether... I let Bobby die to free him or myself."

Cameron's arms tightened around her with his indrawn breath, for that was the truth of it, the dark confession he had been waiting for all this time. He could feel the agony coursing through her with the force of it and it frightened him, because he did not know whether her final admission would free her from the bonds that kept her from him or frighten her into flight again.

Jo Ella did not know, either. And Cameron only held her tighter, because even then, he could feel her slipping away.

Chapter Thirteen

Mary and Burt came to take the baby home. Cam was at work, and Jo Ella knew the apartment would resound with emptiness once they were gone. It did.

They had a full-time housekeeper, the two younger boys were enrolled in day school three days a week, and Mary was continuing in therapy on an outpatient basis. Burt was giving her flying lessons. Mary looked content, in control, and reasonably well adjusted. A good sign was that she could talk about it.

"I didn't really want to die," she confided to Jo Ella as Burt began loading all the baby paraphernalia into the car. "I see that now. It was just—circuit overload. I wanted to do everything by myself, I wouldn't accept the limits that my mind and my body were trying to signal—that I simply couldn't be everything to everyone. And rather than face that"—her smile was regretful, tinged with sorrow—"I chose the easy way out." But then her eyes were clear, her smile steady. "Fortunately, I got a second chance, and I'm going to do it right this time. I don't know, Jo Ella, whether I ever thanked you . . ."

The two women embraced, but within Jo Ella that little knot of fear was tightening and tightening, threatening to cut off her breath.

THE APARTMENT was stripped to its bare beginnings when they were gone, empty and silent. The plants Jo Ella had bought one sunny afternoon a lifetime ago were all dead, and she had not even noticed before this moment. She busied herself with removing the pots from the plant stand, emptying out the dirt and dried foliage and stacking the containers neatly under the sink. But the activity would not quiet her mind, and within her a still desperation was racing and building.

Who was she kidding, anyway? Playing housewife in someone else's home, mother to someone else's child—trying to make herself believe she could insinuate herself into Cam's quiet, settled life and make it belong to her, too. This was not where she belonged. What made her think she could do it? Avis sought escape in the vicarious lives of her soap-opera characters, Mary sought escape... And they were both strong people, people who were settled in their lives and liked them. Jo Ella couldn't expect to succeed where they had failed. Already that restless, breathless yearning was building inside her, already she was looking for open doors.

The empty plant stand in front of the window cast a shadow of interlocking bars on the carpet, like a prison cell. Jo Ella went to the phone and picked up the memo pad on which she had written Albert Jordan's number.

He answered on the third ring. After the usual amenities he said seriously, "I heard about what happened in Austin." Jo Ella's hand clenched on the receiver. "I just want you to know that if I were ever trapped in a hospital room with tubes and machines keeping me alive, I'd hope that there would be a nurse like you around with enough compassion and respect for the dignity of human life to set me free."

Jo Ella closed her eyes slowly and felt the prick of tears behind them. It was one thing to receive the support and forgiveness of family and friends, but to know that there was at least one member of her own profession who had not turned against her, who in fact supported and understood her, was the final benediction. Her voice was a little thick as she said, "Thank you."

He hesitated. "You still have your license, don't you?"

Jo Ella cleared her throat. She knew what was coming. "Yes—I do. But I've almost decided to leave nursing." Almost decided? She had made that decision, firmly, weeks ago. What was she saying? What was she leading herself into?

"I guess it hasn't been easy for you, finding another job."

Jo Ella's laugh was a little stiff. "An understatement."

"It might do you good to get out of the country for a while, to get a perspective on things, before you make a final decision. I'm leaving for Juneau in two weeks, a year-long assignment to train the surgical staff at the corporate medical facility there. I'm not saying that Alaska this time of year would be the answer to your dreams, but I sure could use a good nurse."

Everything within Jo Ella grew very still. Even that awful, nagging pain of uncertainty that had lodged between her ribs for the past week dispersed slowly, and the relief left her lightheaded. Who was she kidding, indeed? It was foolish to try to seek escape in someone else's life—she had to face up to her own responsibilities.

She said, "It sounds like just the thing I've been looking for. When do you need me?"

"Well..." Dr. Jordan sounded relieved, pleased, a little overwhelmed. "I'd like to see you in New York as soon as possible. We have a lot of details to go over and paperwork to clear up before we leave."

Jo Ella said firmly, "I can be on the evening flight and see you first thing in the morning."

That was what Jo Ella had always liked about Dallas—it had one of the largest international airports in the world. She could get a flight out anytime, day or night.

JO ELLA PACKED quickly and efficiently for the flight that was departing for New York at five o'clock. She had brought very little into Cam's life and she would take very little with her—as always, she would not be weighted down with excess baggage. She went directly to the airport, checked her baggage and secured her boarding pass, and there was still plenty of time to make her way across the field to say goodbye to Cam.

She found him in the hangar, stripping down an engine. His coveralls were greasy and his hair was sweaty, the look on his face intent as he wrestled with a wrench and a stubborn bolt. Then he caught her movement out of the corner of his eye and he turned, his face lighting with surprised pleasure. There was a streak of oil across his temple. "Hi," he said, replacing the wrench in the tall toolbox with a clattering sound that echoed off the concrete walls. "What are you doing here?" He started to come toward her, then noticed her white suit and his own greasy hands, and he stopped. But he knew something was wrong before he noticed the suit. Jo Ella could see it in his eyes, in the cautious stance of his body, she could feel it in the air between them, she could hear it in his voice even as he hid behind the easy smile and the casual question. "Did Tiffany get home okay?"

Jo Ella nodded. It was suddenly very, very difficult to speak, and she could feel that breathlessness rising again. What to tell Cam, how to say goodbye? But she had said goodbye to him so many times before, why should this time be any different? She took a deep breath, and it hurt. "Cam," she said, "I'm booked on the five o'clock flight to New York."

Nothing crossed his face. Absolutely nothing. It was as though he had been waiting for those words, hearing them over and over again in his mind, for all of his life. It was no surprise to him. It was inevitable.

He pulled out a soiled blue rag from his back pocket and began to wipe his hands, coming slowly toward her. His eyes were very busy examining the grease stains on his fingers.

Jo Ella went on quickly, just wanting to get it over with, just wanting to get it said and done before she had time to think. "A doctor I once worked with called and offered me a job. It was really too good to turn down, Cam. It's in"—she almost stumbled over the word—"Juneau, Alaska."

Cam nodded. He was standing only a few feet away from her now, but the distance was unbreachable. He smiled, and still his eyes were blank. "Long-term assignment?"

Jo Ella swallowed. "A year."

Cam nodded again, accepting, just as he had always done. Jo Ella felt something rising and tightening in her chest—pain, confusion, frustration or perhaps only the need to be away, to turn her back on the quiet understanding in his eyes that was ripping her apart. A sudden flash came to her of cobalt skies and endless spaces, dusty pecan trees rolling for miles.... Wasn't he going to say anything? What had happened to the house on the edge of the orchard that she had once imagined herself living in, what had happened to quiet nights of desperate loving? *He never made me any promises,* Jo Ella thought. *They were all pipe dreams, they never existed outside my imagination, it was just my way of escaping, and he must have known all along this day would come....*

But, she thought, if he asked her to stay at that moment she might have, she would have—if only he would ask her.

Cam thrust his hands inside the front pockets of his overalls to keep from reaching for her. He knew if he touched her now he would never let her go. Was this it, then? Goodbye, so long, farewell, a scene played out countless times in countless different ways. He would have thought that by now he would be a little better at it. He knew it was coming all along, but somehow he had managed to ignore the inevitable truth these past few weeks, hoping this time it would be different, refusing to believe they were only playing out another interlude in an endless series of interludes. *She never made me any promises,* he thought. There had never been anything to lead him to believe that this time would be any different from the others—and the pain was tearing him apart inside.

Jo Ella said, "Listen, I left my car at your place, and the keys. I wondered—would you mind selling it for me? It's about had it anyway, and there's no point in trying to keep it up. I don't know when..." She let the sentence trail off. Something was breaking inside her, crushing her heart and her lungs, and she did not know how much longer she could drag this thing out.

There was still nothing on Cam's face but the smile that did not reach his eyes. Why didn't he say something? Was he hurting? Was this awful sense of fear and grief and helplessness swallowing him up inside as it was her? Didn't he care? Always before Cam had known exactly the right thing to say, to do, to make everything all right, to put things in perspective and to bring Jo Ella to a clearer sense of herself and her needs. But here and now, at the most important crisis of her life, he was silent.

"Sure thing." It was habit that kept Cam's voice casual, habit that clicked off the switch between the nerve centers in his brain and the tight ball of agony in his chest. Conditioned response. Programming through repetition. He knew exactly what to do. He had had enough practice. "No problem. You'll let me know your address?"

Jo Ella nodded dully, overwhelmed at once by a sense of déjà vu. They had played out this scene before, a different time, a different place, but the lines were the same, the faces were the same—only, perhaps, the feelings were different. She looked at him, and she knew this was it. He was letting her stand on her own, make her own decisions. He had always been there for her, and he had always known when to let her go. She had to do what her needs dictated, and he would not interfere. Only for the first time in her life she was torn between two needs, each as powerful, each as demanding, and she did not know which way to turn.

Jo Ella managed a smile that was a little hopeless, very weak. She didn't know what else to say. "Well... goodbye."

Whatever flickered over Cam's eyes was gone too quickly to give her hope. "Call me before you leave for Alaska," he said. "Keep in touch."

Jo Ella nodded quickly and turned to go. That was it, then. No words of love, no reproaches, no promises. This was Cam, who put no bonds on her, who let her make her own decisions and let her go her own way when she needed to go. Cam, who loved her enough to hold her with open hands.

She did not understand why there were tears in her eyes as she made her way hurriedly back toward the terminal.

CAM LISTENED to the sharp clicking of her heels on the concrete floor and watched her move away from him in that short, aggressive, funny little stride of hers. She had barely rounded the corner before he brought his fist down hard on a work counter, uttering an impotent oath of frustration and fury. His stomach churned and his head throbbed and he berated himself for a fool, but he wasn't sure whether his self-despite came from the weakness that had allowed him to believe in her, or the weakness that had let her go. They were so close this time, so close....

"*Damn,*" he whispered out loud, and he straightened up, dragging his fingers through his hair. Damn it all, he had been so close to having it all in the palm of his hand, and somehow, once again, he had let it slip away.

He stood there with his fists bunched helplessly in his pockets and his eyes narrowed on the place she had been and tried to swallow the anger and the pain and the disappointment he had so carefully refused to let her see. "What're you so upset about?" he muttered out loud, trying to reassure himself with the sound of his own voice. "She'll be back." In a year, or two, she would be back and they would play at this same scenario again, loving each other, holding each other, saying goodbye to each other again.

Maybe it was best. He could have his life back again, settle back into his routine, have everything calm and controlled the way it used to be before Jo Ella had whirled into his life and turned everything upside down. He didn't need the turmoil she had brought, the feeling of helplessness and uncertainty and open-endedness. She had wreaked havoc with his mind, his values, his emotions, just as she always had, just as she always would. She was pushing him beyond the edge of control, and he did not like that feeling.

Control? And what kind of control did he have now,

what kind of life did he have to even want to be in control of when she wasn't here?

"Damn it, is that what you want?" Again he spoke out loud, low, but fiercely. Did he really want to do this to his life? There was no getting over her, no forgetting her, no way not to be there when she needed him, and this insane pattern of hello-goodbye could go on for the rest of his life. And there was no reason except...

Except he kept letting it happen.

For just a moment Cameron hovered on the edge, wrestling with the same insane impulses and fierce drives that had possessed him that day he had made love to her with such abandon in the middle of the field. It was a scary feeling, teetering on the precipice and feeling control slip away, but then he caught a glimpse of how far the fall could be and he did not hesitate any longer. With a sudden determination Cameron threw down the greasy rag and started after her. There were a million things in this world that lay just out of his reach, a thousand closed doors he could not enter and borders over which he could not cross. But Jo Ella was not one of them. And the secret lay in knowing just when to let go.

THE FLIGHT TO NEW YORK was crowded, the plane small. Jo Ella waited until the last call, and even when she got into the line that was shuffling toward the boarding tunnel it was not because she wanted to, but because she felt she had to, almost like a habit. If only he had given her some sign, said something, done something. Or perhaps she could have done something. But what could she say to Cam when he had given her no indication that he wanted her? Cam knew the pattern of their lives, he knew their limitations. He saw it all so much more clearly than she did. He had known from the beginning that Jo Ella could not offer him what he needed, and he did not want her.

The line slowly edged past the gate attendant and into the boarding tunnel. Jo Ella felt a knot of tension uncertainly, anxiously settle in her solar plexus. What was she doing? What kind of imaginary debt was she trying to settle now? She did not want to go to Alaska, she didn't want to go back to nursing. Once she had run away from the ghost of Bobby Williams; was she now running away from what she perceived to be her failure of Mary?

No. That was stupid. That was insane. Jo Ella steeled her nerves and moved past the gate attendant, closer to the tunnel. This had nothing to do with Mary, nothing at all.

But it did. It had to do with Mary's failure as a wife and a mother and a human being, and Jo Ella's fear of the same. It had to do with the fact that Jo Ella still felt as though she had let it happen, because she had not seen it coming or been able to prevent it. And what was she doing now? She was taking responsibility for the whole world on her shoulders, and that responsibility was too much for her, it scared her. She was making the same mistake Mary had. She was taking the easy way out.

Jo Ella moved into the tunnel with the rest of the crowd, elbows jostling her and carry-on luggage bumping her, and for just a minute she experienced a familiar surge of rising breathlessness, of panic, of helplessness.

It was the same feeling she had had just before she had made that telephone call to Albert Jordan.

Jo Ella stood still, frozen not by fear, but by a sudden overwhelming bolt of clarity. Less than three hours ago she had stood at the edge of a precipice with her own doubts and fears and inadequacies clamoring at her, pummeling her, crowding her and taking away her breath; she had panicked, just as she always did, and she saw her only option as flight. If she had thought about it for even one minute she might have considered other alternatives. But she hadn't thought about it at all.

Jo Ella turned around, murmuring apologies to the disgruntled passengers behind her, trying to push her way past them. There was anxiety racing in her chest now, but it wasn't the smothering kind; her heart was pounding and her palms were sweating, but it wasn't from fear, it was from something almost like hope. She knew it was crazy. She knew he didn't want her. *Then I'll make him want me.* She knew she did not belong in his life, she had only been living out a fantasy. *We'll make our own life, together, a place where we both belong.* She was not Mary; she would not make the same mistakes. She knew her limits. She could make the fantasy a reality, for when it came down to it the only place she had ever really escaped to was the safety of Cam's arms—all her life, flying in an endless circle that led her straight back to him.

There was a disturbance up ahead to match the one Jo Ella was creating behind her as she pushed her way back through the tunnel. There were angry voices and shuffling noises, and then Jo Ella's heart gave a viable jerk as she thought she heard her name called. The engines were roaring in her ears and she couldn't be sure, but there it was again. It was Cam's voice.

She stopped, her heart leaping to her throat and renewing its frantic rhythm there, and other heads were turning behind her in the crowded tunnel that led from the gate to the plane, voices were murmuring, and then there was a shriek or two, a definite argument at the end of the line. Jo Ella heard, quite clearly now, "Joey—wait!" And she started to push her way through the crowd again, her heart filling up her chest and her ears, and she couldn't believe it, but there he was, pushing his way up through the line as she pushed her way back, shouting to her—and above the numb, paralyzing joy that propelled her through the bodies crushing her toward him, she kept thinking, insanely, *I can't believe it, Cam is making a scene!*

People were shouting more angrily now, scowling at him, there was an occasional feminine cry of alarm as Cam pushed intrepidly past, and then suddenly Cam was grabbed from behind by a uniformed guard; Jo Ella's hand flew to her throat and she lost sight of Cam in the scuffle that ensued. Now there was much jostling and crying out as everyone tried to get a glimpse of what was going on, someone was shrieking behind her, "It's a hijacker—oh, my God!" and the stewardess was trying to make her way through the mass, calling, "Will everyone calm down please? Everything is under control.... What *is* going on here?"

Jo Ella was pushing and shoving, trying to reach him, and she got pushed and shoved and knocked off balance in return. Then her arm was grabbed and she was whirled around, and it was Cam, holding her.

For a moment they just stared at each other. His face was grim, his hair disheveled. His left eye and cheekbone were purplish red and already beginning to swell, and there was a trickle of blood at the corner of his mouth. He was breathing hard, and his grip on her arm was fierce. Then he gave her a short jerk and began to drag her through the crowd, pushing bodies out of his way, past the huddle at the door where a uniformed man was moaning against the wall, into the light near the gate. There he stopped, holding her by both arms, tightly, turning her to face him. Jo Ella's shocked eyes went from the injured man to Cam's battered face, and she couldn't believe it. Cam had fought for her. Cam had actually hit a man. The look in his eyes was quietly desperate. "Damn it, Jo Ella, I know I have no right to do this," he said, his voice harsh and low, his breath coming in short gasps, "I'm not asking you to stay—I can't make you do that, but I can go with you. I can't let this keep on happening to us, I can't let you walk away again."

Jo Ella could say nothing, she could only bring a trembling hand up to wipe away the blood from Cam's lip, but the sheer shock and wonder of it all made her arm too weak to maintain even that brief contact His words showered over her with quick intensity, pelting her like determined raindrops on arid earth, and his fingers dug into her arms "Don't you see that we're always going to be together?" he demanded hoarsely "We've just been wasting time, precious time, pretending otherwise. It doesn't matter whether it's in Texas or Juneau or Mars. For God's sake, Joey, we can't do this again!"

Jo Ella felt breath infused into her body through lips that were parted in wonder, but it was still too much for her to believe. She couldn't speak, she could only raise her hands to his throat, fingers stretching to caress his neck, holding him, hoping he could read her eyes. He scanned her face and then his own face softened, and so did the grip on her arms, but it was as though he, too, was having difficulty believing what he saw there. There was tenderness in his voice, pleading for her understanding, but also an uncertainty, a hope he could not quite express.

"Joey, don't you know you're the other part of me?" His voice was so husky now it was almost a whisper. "When you leave me you take all that's real and vital and alive with you. We need each other, Joey. You need me to keep your feet on the ground and I need you to remind me to dream. If you leave, you'll be tearing both of us in half." His hand came up, unsteadily, and cupped her face. His eyes were filled with such love, such gentleness, that Jo Ella felt her heart constrict and begin to melt. There was still uncertainty there, and desperate hope, but from far within the depths of his eyes he even coaxed a smile. "Besides," he said softly, "who's going to hold your hand in the tunnel?"

Jo Ella stepped against him, burying her face in his rough-textured, greasy-smelling coverall; she tightened her arms around him as his tightened around her, and she did not know how she would get the words out beyond the lump of sheer joy that was in her throat. "I was coming back to you," she whispered. "I started to get on the plane and I just couldn't. I don't know why you want me—you know you're not getting much in me—but you're all I've ever wanted, Cam, I've always come back to you and I just couldn't leave you again. Oh, Cam, why did you let it get this far? Why didn't you stop me?"

She lifted her face to him, and she saw the stark relief and rising wonder in his eyes that seemed to widen and brighten and for a moment blot out everything but the two of them, together, and the miracle of it. Then, as the noise and confusion all around them spiraled them slowly back into the world of reality, a spark of teasing came into his eyes. "I thought," he informed her wryly, "that was what I was doing."

Jo Ella lightly, in disbelief, brushed her fingers across the rapidly darkening bruise on Cam's cheek. He winced. "You fought for me," she said, wonder in her voice.

He looked around—at the guard who was just staggering to his feet behind them, at the gate attendant who was nursing a bruised jaw—and he murmured with a stab of regret, "I guess I let myself get a little out of control. Now you know why I don't fight." And he smiled at her, an unsteady hand lightly touching her hair. "This time," he told her gently, "I think getting out of control was the best thing that could have happened to me."

They both turned at the sound of feet running across the tile floor, and Jo Ella saw the stunned look of weary acceptance cross Cam's face at the approach of two guards, their faces grim, their hands on their holsters. "Good God," he said quietly, "I think I'm going to jail."

Jo Ella laughed out loud, partially from sheer happiness, partially from the look of comic disbelief on Cam's face when he mentally reviewed his own rash actions of only moments ago and began to resolve the reality of the consequences with such unprecedented behavior. "Don't worry," she assured him. "I'll bake you a cake with a file in it."

Cam glanced at her ruefully as the guards drew ever nearer. "If you really loved me," he said, "you'd go with me."

Jo Ella looked at him, and all the love and all the tenderness she had ever felt for him, and would feel for him for the rest of her life, was reflected in her eyes. "I think you always knew," she told him softly, "that all you had to do was reach out your hand to me and I would put mine in it."

Cam looked at her, and Jo Ella knew he was not seeing her as she stood before him in a crowded airport boarding gate with curious, suspicious and hostile people all around them and two guards with guns bearing down on them. He was seeing her as she stood poised in a hayloft or on a metal roof, he was seeing her on a bicycle and roller skates, in cap and gown on graduation day, he was seeing her running into his arms and waving goodbye; he was seeing her over a candlelit table and lying in the grass on the edge of a pecan orchard with sun in her hair and arms open to him. And he was seeing her on the terrace of an as-yet-unbuilt house with the sunset spilling over her, turning to greet him, he was seeing her climbing a tree with a little girl who looked amazingly like her, he was seeing her running through fields with her laughter in the wind and himself at her heels...he was seeing her with gray in her hair and light in her eyes as he came through the door. And he inquired, softly, "Just like that?"

Cam opened his hand to her and Jo Ella's hand closed around it. "Just like that," she answered.

Readers rave about Harlequin American Romance!

"...the best series of modern romances I have read...great, exciting, stupendous, wonderful."

—S.E., Coweta, Oklahoma*

"...they are absolutely fantastic...going to be a smash hit and hard to keep on the bookshelves."

—P.D., Easton, Pennsylvania

"The American line is great. I've enjoyed every one I've read so far."

—W.M.K., Lansing, Illinois

"...the best stories I have read in a long time."

—R.H., Northport, New York

**Names available on request.*